A GRATEFUL KISS

"Georgi? Georgi, speak to me . . ."

"What can I say?" she muttered. "What can I say? You saved my life."

Another fear clutched at Everhart. Would she marry him out of gratitude? He didn't want that. "Th. . . . . . Be-

BOOKS BY JEANNE SAVERY

The Widow and the Rake

A Reformed Rake

A Christmas Treasure

A Lady's Deception

Cupid's Challenge

Lady Stephanie

A Timeless Love

A Lady's Lesson

Lord Galveston and the Ghost

A Lady's Proposal

The Widowed Miss Mordaunt

A Love for Lydia

Taming Lord Renwick

Lady Serena's Surrender

The Christmas Gift

The Perfect Husband

A Perfect Match

Smuggler's Heart

Miss Seldon's Suitors

An Independent Lady

The Family Matchmaker

Published by Zebra Books

THE FAMILY MATCHMAKER

Jeanne Savery

Zebra Books
Kensington Publishing Corp.
http://www.kensingtonbooks.com

One

"Well! You've gotten yourself into a right pickle, have you not, my child?"

Startled, Georgianna Thomasina clutched the angel Gabriel's stone skirts and looked down at the stranger who had appeared from nowhere. *Drat!* It was too bad, she thought, but, most likely, it had been a futile hope that no one would find her before her grandfather finished inside the parish church and returned to help her down from her perch on the golden Cotswold stone plinth. Georgi kicked one heel against the statue's base. Why had she chosen today to climb up to scrub off her old favorite Gabriel, who secured one side of the church entrance while St. George stood guard over the other. Georgi had never had a fondness for St. George—perhaps because everyone in her family was named George in some form or other.

But the stranger had said *child,* had he not? Perhaps she could, even now, get out of this without too much embarrassment.

"What are you doing up there?" he asked, tipping his curly brimmed beaver farther back on his head. He stared up at her.

"How would you feel if a silly old bird sat on your head?" she asked by way of answer. Ahh! When he grinned like that, his eyes narrowed in such a nice way, she thought.

"I wouldn't like it at all. Especially if it left its, hmm," he quirked an eyebrow, "calling card?"

She sighed a soft blissful sigh at his instant understanding. "Well, it did, then."

"So?"

"So, last Sunday, I promised poor old Gabriel I'd clean him up. But, sometimes, it isn't easy to keep promises. This is the first opportunity I've had."

"You've done a good job, too," he said, looking approvingly around the well-scrubbed figure. "So why don't you come down now?"

Georgi kicked her foot again. Then she wished she hadn't when she noticed how the raising of her skirts gave the stranger a glimpse of her ankles, an opportunity he didn't waste. Perhaps he wasn't a gentleman after all.

"Well?" he insisted, his lips twitching when she tucked the skirts around her.

"Well, I can't."

The man didn't quite manage to hide a chuckle. "What will you give me, pretty little maid, if I help you down?"

Her eyes widened. So? He didn't think her a child after all? Worse, the blasted man must think her a village girl and fair game, as her cousin George Elliot would say in his sneering way. George Vincent, her favorite cousin, would purse his lips and, pedantically, correct "the fellow's" misapprehension before he'd order the stranger to take himself off. . . . Then, of course, when they were alone, he and Georgi would enjoy the joke! How she missed George Vincent and wished he'd come for a visit. Georgi sighed.

"Well, child? Would I get a kiss for my pains?"

She tipped her head to a prim, nose-in-the-air, height. "I'll wait for my grandfather, thank you just the same."

"Your grandfather helped you up there?"

"No." Georgi heaved an exasperated sigh. "A *ladder* helped me up. Those pesky Reeves twins stole it away," she added before he could ask "What ladder?" as she knew he would. Then, before he could ask the *next* logical question, she said, "Grandfather is in the church." The man was just full of questions, she thought, and wondered if she were, once again, setting herself beyond the pale (as Aunt Anne—*Georgina* Anne—would insist) by talking to the man at all. "Umm? I'm sorry, I didn't hear that," she said crossly, having missed his comment while thinking about her more severe aunt's strictures on her behavior.

"Your grandfather. He's the beadle perhaps?"

Georgi stifled a giggle behind a too-tanned hand. "No sir," she managed, but it was a trifle strangled by the ill-controlled laughter. "Not—not—the beadle."

"Then what's he doing in there on a weekday?"

"Praying that Farmer George will, once again, return to his senses so that the poor man's profligate son need not be made Regent after all."

The stranger's brows snapped together. Very fine brows they were, too, she thought. Just right for showing anger, for arching questioningly, for doing all sorts of wonderful things she'd never been able to get her own brows to do when practicing before her mirror. It was a bore how very uncooperative her brows could be.

When he didn't speak, she said, "Grandfather's a *very* strong supporter of the King."

"What's your name?" he asked sharply.

The man was, she noted, still frowning. "I'm Georgianna Thomasina," she replied. "Grandfather named us all George—or a variation of it."

"I presume you also have a last name?"

She eyed him. "I don't believe I'll tell you that."

He paused, but accepted her rather belated attempt at propriety, such as it was, and returned to an earlier question. "You never told me what you'd give me if I got you down."

The brows had a flirtatious tilt now, she thought. How could he think her a child and still flirt with her? Or maybe someone fifteen or so *was* a child in his eyes, although still available for dallying? Was it at all possible her Aunt Anne was right in saying she must not speak to strangers? Ah well. It was too late now.

"Well? What would you?" he urged.

"What would I? Why, I'd call out to my grandfather to come thank you properly for your kind rescue."

"The devil you would!"

"On Gabriel's wings I swear it." She patted the stone figure's knee.

"Do you not fear your grandfather will scold if he finds you up there?"

"He'll scold, but his eyes will twinkle. He'll think it a great joke."

"*Joke.*" The scowl was back. "He'll think it a *joke* his granddaughter is up there where she may be accosted by any loose screw who wanders by?"

"A person such as yourself, perhaps?" asked a mild voice, this one from the entryway to the church. "Why *are* you up there, Georgi?" She explained again. "That is not your duty, child. If it worried you, you should have told me to tell the verger to care for it. Did you say why you are *still* up there?"

"It was those Reeves twins, Grandfather."

"Ah. It is always those Reeves twins, is it not? And where, my child, do you suppose they put the ladder?"

"Behind Miss Hipplewyte's slab," responded Georgi promptly.

"Hmm. So I see."

The stranger moved quickly. "I'll get it, sir."

"It's more proper," said Georgi from her perch, "to say 'my lord.'"

The stranger swung around, the end of the ladder barely missing the top of the Appledore monument. His gaze went from Georgianna, idly swinging her foot, to the stiff-backed old gentleman he'd obviously taken for a retired military man or some such. Grandfather, noticed Georgianna—and not for the first time—also had an interesting trick with his eyebrows. Only *he* managed it with only one. The younger man moved forward, placed the ladder firmly, and, with belated attention to propriety, turned his back.

Georgianna maneuvered her skirts in a practiced manner and climbed down. "Thank you, sir," she said, once both her feet were firmly on the ground.

There was an exceedingly dry note in the stranger's voice when he responded, "You might, more properly, say 'my lord.'" He bowed. "Lord Everhart, at your service."

Georgi blushed. *That's torn it,* she thought. *Aunt Marie will have hysterics and Aunt Anne won't stop scolding for a seven-day.* "My grandfather, Lord Tivington," she said, her voice sounding odd in her ears as she attempted to restrain imminent giggles.

"And yourself?" he asked after exchanging stiffly proper words with the old man whose green-brown eyes *did* twinkle. Rather disconcerting they were too. "Miss . . . ?"

Georgi looked to her grandfather. He nodded very slightly. "Miss Georgianna Thomasina Beverly." She curtsied. It was not one of her better efforts, since her mind was occupied elsewhere.

Imagine bantering words as she'd done with one she now knew to be of the Prince's set. Assuming she'd heard correctly, that is, when her Aunt Marie—Aunt *Georgia* Marie—read from the society columns. So, very likely he was a notorious gambler and rake, and, if he was the one she thought he was, he was a well-known collector. *That* much she remembered, *but a collector of what?*

Perhaps she should listen more closely when her society-minded Aunt Marie read from the society pages? Then she'd know what it was this tall man with the mobile eyebrows collected. At the moment she very much feared it might be hearts! She turned her gaze to her grandfather, pleading with him.

His lordship quirked a brow. "We must be off now. You are, I presume, at Minnow Manor?" Everhart nodded. "Then I think you should join us this evening for potluck, my lord. Assuming, that is, that you don't mind the country hour of six?"

Georgi hid a smile behind her hand at the alacrity with which the invitation was accepted but frowned at the notion they'd meet again so soon. Lord Everhart was too unsettling for words and she needed time to put her mind in order—to say nothing of her wayward emotions. She and her grandfather were well away before she asked if Lord Everhart had inherited the Manor.

"I expected he'd be the heir when Sir Minnow died. I am surprised, however, that he's come himself to inspect it."

"The Season is over, is it not?" This fact she'd gathered from Aunt Marie's conversation.

Actually, Georgi couldn't have escaped the information. Aunt Marie had gone on at length bemoaning that her niece had not been presented during the Season and now it was over and the child would very likely die a spinster, which was *not* the most pleasant thing in the world as who knew better than herself . . . and much more of the same.

"That is the case, is it not?" she asked again when he didn't respond.

"Hmm? You asked . . . ? Oh," said her grandfather. "Yes, the Season in London has ended, but Everhart and his ilk should, by now, be disporting themselves along the Styne in Brighton."

Brighton. "Isn't that where the Prince has his summer residence?"

"The Pavilion, yes."

"And Lord Everhart is a great friend of the Prince?"

"He is."

Georgi turned her head sideways for a quick glance at her grandfather's stern face. "Grandfather . . ."

"Yes, child?"

Georgi's frown deepened. "If he is the Prince's man, why did you invite him to dinner?"

Old eyes twinkled down at her, thin old lips compressed against a chuckle. Then one mobile eyebrow rose in a stern arc. "Have *you* ever been forced to eat a meal prepared by the Manor's Mrs. Gates?"

Georgi admitted she had not.

"If you *had,* you'd not ask that question. Mrs. Gates cannot cook." The old man continued with that dry note Georgi knew so well. "My invitation was in sympathy for my fellow man and would have been given if Everhart were a dastard of the lowest breed, which, to be truthful, I do not believe him to be, despite his adherence to the Prince's set. I could not leave a dog to suffer Mrs. Gates's cooking so long as I'd a crust of my own to share." Lord Tivington touched his granddaughter's arm with his cane, halting her. He stared down at her. "I have just had a somewhat worrying thought."

"Yes, Grandfather?" she asked when he didn't continue.

"You. *You,* my dear, have reached an age to marry, which fact has been dinned into my ears the last two years by both your aunts. I have ignored their importuning because, to my mind, you've shown none of the signs by which a girl exhibits an interest in men and the setting up of her own home. Be that as it may, you *are* of an age to interest Lord Everhart, at least to the extent he may wish to set up a flirtation. You will oblige me by ignoring any effort he makes in that direction. It is not that I do not trust him to behave as a gentleman, Georgi," he went on to explain. "You are not a mere nobody with whom he may safely trifle. But he *may,* very easily, do damage of which he is unaware."

"Damage?" she asked when, again, he paused in his speech. If she'd had a mirror just then, she'd have been exceedingly proud of the behavior of her *own* left eyebrow. It often arched quite nicely when she wasn't trying and at that moment did it very well.

"You are very young, my child . . ."

"Grandfather, *I am very nearly twenty.*" She couldn't suppress the annoyed tone. It was a great deal too bad, really. Unless one knew her great age, one would never guess it, so slight and small as she was. Lord Everhart hadn't. It was the bane of her existence that she looked more a boy than a girl, when her cousin, who was *months* younger, had looked the woman for years now. "My birthday is next month, as you well know!"

"Oh, a great age, to be sure." She blushed and he touched her cheek lightly. "However old you are in years, you're a babe when it comes to men and their ways. Such men are rakes, my dear. Do you know what *that* means?"

"Well, when James was required to marry Betty . . ."

"Harrumph." Lord Tivington's ears reddened. The reason for the quick wedding of the upstairs maid and first footman should *not* have come to his granddaughter's innocent ears.

"But Aunt Anne said . . ."

"Enough. You have a notion, at least, of my meaning. A man of his lordship's stripe will not do for you, my dear. He is, in experience, a hundred years beyond you. Do not lose your foolish heart to him. If he is bored, as he is certain to be, he will look about him for distraction. You, Georgi, have turned into a surprisingly charming young woman. Your innocence *should* protect you from the man—I believe it will or I'd not invite him to our home in spite of my pity for him—but what he will *not* understand is that you've no experience of the light, nonsensical, and ever meaningless flirtation which is so much a part of his world. I fear you'll take him seriously." Again he stopped her with his cane. "You must not, my child."

"I must not fall in love with him," she said dutifully. "But isn't that mostly because he's the Prince's man and not the King's?"

"I suppose that, too, plays a part in my thinking," said her grandfather stiffly. A sadness enveloped him like an almost visible miasma as he continued. "If that were all I could not forbid you to him. The world must change. A new era is, despite my dislike of it, rushing upon us. The enclosures in the country, the manufactories in the midlands, the war . . . With luck," he said, sighing, "I'll not live to see much more of it . . ."

"Grandfather!" Georgi snatched at his arm, jerked it when he didn't immediately look at her. Their eyes met, identical green-brown eyes with long lashes and the faintest of tilts to the corners. "Grandfather! Don't!"

"Child?" He removed her clutching fingers from his sleeve. "Why such heat?"

"Don't *say* such things. Don't even *think* them! You are not an old man. You are perfectly healthy. You mustn't . . ."

His hand stopped the flood of words, which were rising in timbre and tone. "Child, I will not leave you unprotected." His brows closed together into a thoughtful line. "But perhaps your aunts have the right of it? Perhaps it *is* time I looked about me for a husband for you?"

Georgi's lips compressed. "I don't want a husband."

"Not at all?" he asked with a smile.

"No. Not at all."

The smile disappeared into a frown. "Why?"

She eyed him, then looked to where her toe dug into the dirt of the path. She pointed her toe and stared at her slipper. Her Aunt Anne would scold at the scraped place in the soft leather. . . .

"Why, child?" insisted Lord Tivington.

"I just don't," she mumbled.

He forced her chin up, compelling her eyes to meet his. Very sternly he asked her, "Georgianna, has someone told you . . . something . . . which has frightened you?"

"About having babies?" Her cheeks reddened. "It sounds unpleasant, but I don't think I'm afraid." She turned aside, the red deepening almost to puce. "Neither to have one nor, hmm, to make one. No. It isn't that."

Lord Tivington hid a smile. Somehow, Georgianna had acquired information which her prim and proper aunts would very likely prefer hidden from their niece—even if it meant the two of them agreeing for a change! "Then . . . ?"

"Do I have to tell you?"

"Would I not understand?"

"Oh, Grandfather, you always understand. It's just that it's silly and unworthy, and, well, I suppose, a trifle selfish . . ."

The old gentleman searched his mind. The single brow rose. "You fear he will not allow you the freedom that I have allowed you?"

"That's part . . ."

"You think he'll forbid you his library, perhaps?"

She paled. "I couldn't bear it, Grandfather!"

"Do you think I'd allow you to wed a man ashamed of your mind, of your talent for"—he glanced around—"writing novels?"

"But," she whispered, also looking around, "you said we may not tell even *the aunts* that fact."

"That's different."

She tipped her head, staring at him. "Grandfather, do you truly think you can find me a husband who will be just like you?"

He chuckled, pleased by the flattery hidden in her question. He tweaked her nose. Tipping his head, he asked, "Now why would you want a man like your old grandfather?"

"Because he'd be a man who makes me laugh and because he wouldn't scold—much—when I get into scrapes and because he'd encourage me to be myself and not a pattern card of propriety like my cousin, George Cassie. *Would* you scold if I tell you I think George Cassie a very silly young woman?"

"Since I agree with you I don't have a right to scold. However I *will* scold you for not calling her by her proper name. She is Georgette Cassandra, my dear, and . . ." His brows snapped together. "Blast and bedamned!"

Georgi put her hand to her mouth, her eyes widening. They'd forgotten her grandfather's heir's wife and daughter were to arrive that very day. Suddenly she laughed. "Oh, Grandfather, you were concerned Lord Everhart might wish to flirt with *me!* With Cassie about, he'll not so much as *look* at me." Georgi wondered why that thought made her chest tighten and her eyes burn. She didn't *want* Lord Everhart to flirt with her. Did she?

"I promised Georgina Anne we'd be home to greet them. Since your Aunt Melicent and your cousin have very likely arrived, I've broken my promise."

"Dinna fratch yourself, milord," said Georgi, deepening her voice in imitation of his lordship's longtime valet. "Dinna worry your haid, noo. Just let That Woman learn an eligible lord will be setting his looong legs 'neath your dinner table, milord, and she'll niver notice you failed to greet her on her arrival."

"How truly you speak, child," said her grandfather bitingly, "but in future may I suggest you sound more like a young lady and a Beverly?" Lord Tivington turned and walked swiftly along the path, his cane stabbing into it with each step. Georgi ran to catch him up. "But perhaps," he said hopefully, "something slowed their carriage. With luck we may yet return in time. I do not care to give my head for washing when it is Georgina Anne who will use the scrub brush! She goes on and on and it is more than flesh and blood should be made to bear. Come, child," he added. "Don't dawdle."

Late afternoon sun streamed in the west windows of the master bedroom at Minnow Manor. "Well, Hamish?" Lord Everhart stared into the badly spotted mirror. "Will I do?"

"I believe so, m'lord. Lord Tivington is a proper old gentleman. I'm quite certain he still dresses for dinner as he did in his youth."

Everhart's brows drew into a line. "He wore his hair

pulled back in a queue, but it was definitely his own hair."

"Very likely, m'lord. And very likely he no longer powders it even for the evening. But he will don knee breeches and rings and all the rest when he dresses for dinner. Just the one ring, perhaps?" wheedled the valet.

"I am not of my lord Tivington's generation. He'll not expect me to appear dressed as if it were my intention to continue on to Almack's. Leave it, Hamish," he added when the valet would have given him a last brushing-down. "Why did I agree to this? A country evening amongst countrified souls who will very likely think they give me a high treat when they suggest playing whist for penny points—and *that* after we've eaten far too much for comfort!"

"Which is just what you will enjoy," said Hamish a trifle severely. When Everhart's brows rose, the valet added, *"Not* eating to satiation, m'lord, but you know very well you are not one for deep doings at table and turf. Playing a friendly game of whist will be a pleasure."

"Very true. The only reason the Prince tolerates me is that we enjoy adding to our collections of fine Oriental china and exchanging information—that is a polite way of saying we brag, of course—concerning our latest acquisitions."

"When he isn't asking your advice concerning a sale or," grumbled Hamish, whose loyalty was firmly to his master, "asking you to acquire something for him."

For which, thought Everhart sourly, *he then forgets to pay me.*

Everhart was not a poor man but neither was he so wealthy he could afford many such gifts to the Crown, which was one reason he'd decided to look over this un-expected inheritance from Sir Minnow, a relative of such tenuous relationship he'd not yet determined exactly where they met on the family tree. The inspection would keep him from Brighton and from Prinny's demands for a month or two and for that he was thankful. Absently he accepted gloves, cane, and lace-edged handkerchief. Realizing what he held, he handed back the handkerchief and cane.

"Hamish . . ."

"Yes m'lord?"

"Don't try that innocent act on *me*."

"Yes, m'lord." Hamish frowned. "Or do I mean no, m'lord?"

"I haven't a notion what you mean, but what *I* mean is that, if you don't cease tricking me out like a demned caper merchant, I'll have to let you go."

"Yes, m'lord."

Everhart eyed the man's solemn face. He sighed. "You are incorrigible."

"Very likely, m'lord." Hamish bowed, his nose very nearly touching his knees.

Lord Everhart laughed as he'd been meant to do and went through the door which creaked when opened for him. So, too, would the steps of the main staircase when he walked down them. Could he *bear* living here for the weeks necessary for discovering what was needed to set things to rights? As he stood at the top of the badly polished staircase leading down to the dark and dreary main hall, the hinges to the door to his room squealed again.

"Hamish, add the soaping of all hinges to the list we've made, will you please?"

His lordship allowed himself to be driven to Tivingtons' in Sir Minnow's old carriage. He hadn't ridden in a vehicle so badly sprung since he was a tad of a boy and been taken here and there by his doting grandmother. A further note was added to the growing list of things of immediate necessity: his own carriage must be sent for along with more horses. Horses were another of the many things to which his ancient relative had paid scant attention. Lord Everhart reached for the strap and gripped it tightly to keep himself from bouncing off the seat. With luck, he thought wryly, he might actually reach Beverly Place without losing a wheel or breaking an axle. He wondered if it was worth it.

As they traversed the Cotswold lanes, he reviewed his meeting with Miss Beverly. Had the hoyden amused him or had she not? She was such an innocent—or was she artful in the extreme? Surely her grandfather, at least, recognized his name and knew of the reputation which association with Prinny gave one. In his case it was undeserved, but the earl couldn't know that, and must believe him a rake, a wastrel, and untrustworthy. So why the instant invitation to dine? Were there so few eligibles in the neighborhood Lord Tivington would look to any man to rid him of the minx? But then, wasn't the child too young to think of wedding? Then again, country misses married young, and even if the area were as full as it could hold of young men, they might be too wary of Miss Beverly's obvious waywardness to offer for her—however amusing that same waywardness might be.

Everhart's inner monologue came to an end as Sir Minnow's coachman drew his pair to a halt before a neat, quite simple, but surprisingly impressive, mansion. Two short flights of steps separated by a narrow paved terrace led to the double front door. The entrance was protected by no more than a shallow roof, but its angle was echoed by a much larger extension of the main roof three stories above. The pediment of the larger roof was held up by four monstrous ionic columns set close to the house. On each floor identical windows gleamed between the columns. Very simple but very effective lines to the house, with wings extending to either side of the central structure. It was a good, solid mansion, likely built not more than forty to fifty years ago.

Everhart, however, preferred the olio of styles, assembled through several centuries, which was his own home. Odd corners and varying ceiling heights led to the necessity of unexpected steps here and there along the corridors; it was in constant need of repair, had drainage problems, and was often uncomfortably cold in the older portions during winter storms. Still, despite all that, Everhart wished he were in Devonshire at Heartland, preparing to eat in the Elizabethan dining room, with its low beams and mellow candlelight. Instead, he would very likely find himself staring at a picture of dead hares and ripe cheeses hung on the wall across from his seat at table. It was a style of art he abominated.

Lord Everhart made all the proper noises to Lord Tivington, who came into the hall at his arrival. They were still speaking when the butler returned to the dining room, where he was making a last check that all was ready for the main meal of the day. They heard his soft fussing about drapes that had not been pulled, a duty forgotten by the youngest footman, who had not quite got the hang of things. The two men grinned at each other, both knowing the problems of training a new servant and the oddities of service one must endure while that was in progress.

Despite that moment of shared humor, Everhart entered the drawing room wondering how he'd manage to survive an evening of extreme boredom. One look around the room and he very nearly turned tail and ran.

His difficulty would not be surviving boredom, but countering the machinations of a woman he should have guessed would be visiting her father-in-law.

It was no secret Everhart would not be in Brighton that summer. Nor was it a secret he'd inherited a property from his reclusive relative, Sir Minnow. It did not take the intelligence which existed in Lady Melicent's cockloft to put the two together and come up with a very accurate four. The only question now was whether old Tivington was involved in the lady's plots to entrap him for her beautiful featherhead of a daughter. He must immediately put a spoke in the lady's wheel or he'd find himself run in circles by mother and daughter!

As his thoughts raced, he did the polite thing by the spinster aunts, Lady Georgia Marie Beverly and Lady Georgina Anne, and nodded toward Lady Melicent's son, Elliot Beverly, about whom he'd heard too much and little of it good. He bowed to Lady Melicent and her daughter, Cassandra, murmuring that they'd not met for some weeks, and, as soon as introductions were finished turned to where the child, Georgianna Thomasina Beverly, sat just a little out of the way. He picked up a chair and moved it a foot nearer to her.

"Did you survive your adventure, Miss Beverly?"

"Adventure?" intruded Elliot's sneering voice.

The high tenor was an irritant. With that irritation showing, Everhart looked up at the young man. "Merely a manner of speaking, Beverly. Merely a manner of speaking." He felt the young woman beside him relax. "And *your* last adventure?" he asked the younger man. "I see you've survived your brush with disaster, but, that is *not* in a manner of speaking, is it?"

Young George Elliot Beverly reddened and scowled. "I don't care to be reminded, my lord."

"Oh, but *I'd* like to hear," said Georgi. "Do tell, Lord

Everhart. Elliot is forever teasing me and preaching at me and grossly exaggerating my escapades. I would dearly love to know of one of his with which I may retaliate!"

"I do not think . . ." Elliot began in his mincing way when Lord Everhart interrupted him.

"Mr. Beverly had the ill luck to fall into the hands of a card sharper. I believe his mother and father were not pleased with him."

Georgi's eyes widened. *"Now* I understand why you are rusticating, George Elliot. You are *not* merely escorting your sister and mother as you led the aunts to believe. I thought you were telling a bouncer when I saw the trunks hauled up to your room. If you were only escorting them, you would have turned tail immediately and returned to London or on to Brighton or wherever one goes this time of year." Georgi scowled. "I might have known you were here to stay." She eyed him speculatively, her eyes glittering. "Now, what will we *do* with you? I can't *think* how you'll survive a sojourn in the country."

"You hold that knife-edged tongue of yours, Georgianna Thomasina. I'll not have a chit of a female with more hair than wit, no experience of the World, and far too blue to be accepted by anyone of any consequence tell *me* what I think or do or have . . ."

"Got your mouth going again, have you, grandson?" asked Lord Tivington mildly. "I thought you'd outgrown that tendency to spout off."

"Then tell *her*—" George Elliot gestured toward Georgi. "—to keep her tongue off what she knows nothing about. Everhart, promise me a game of piquet after dinner, will you?"

"I believe," said Lord Tivington, dangerously polite, "your aunts have plans. We may make up two whist tables if all play." He held his grandson's eyes, a severity he seldom displayed evident. "Your aunts enjoy whist a great deal, George Elliot, and too rarely have the opportunity to play with new acquaintances."

Elliot mumbled something about chicken-stakes and old-fashioned long whist rather than the modern short style he preferred and turned away. His place was taken by the golden-haired beauty of the family, Cassandra, who had just finished her third Season unbetrothed and unwed. She was a major danger to Everhart's peace of mind. Pretending he didn't see her, he looked directly into Georgi's eyes and asked if she'd partner him at whist.

"Thank you, my lord, but I believe my Aunt Marie is looking forward to that pleasure. She spent half an hour arranging the tables, so I do not feel I can upset her decisions by obliging you, my lord."

"Will you at least be at my table, Miss Beverly?"

"Part of the evening, my lord. You know very well how one progresses, changing tables, as one plays," she chided before realizing he'd begun the expected flirtation. But why was it with *her* and *not* with her golden-haired beauty of a cousin?

"Do I hear a reprimand?"

"If you do," she scolded, "I daresay you deserve it."

He chuckled. "I believe that may be your butler announcing dinner. May I take you in, Miss Beverly?" He held his arm for Georgi to take. After a glance at her grandfather, she obliged.

"Come, Georgette Cassandra," said the old man. "I will honor myself by taking you in to dinner. We will not stand on formality since the men are so outnumbered by the women." He offered his other arm to Lady Melicent, suggested Everhart do the same for his elder daughter, and ordered George Elliot to take in his other aunt.

When they arrived at the table, the old gentleman proceeded to appoint the seating arrangements as well. Lady Melicent gnashed her teeth when she saw her daughter placed as far from Lord Everhart as it was possible to seat her. Her only consolation was that Georgi was also placed away from the eligible parti who, although not so rich as Lady Melicent would prefer, would, under the circumstances, do well enough for Cassandra.

Dinner was not a success. It was, however, a far better tasting meal than Everhart had had from Sir Minnow's old retainers. Something must be done about that, too. He couldn't very well eat every meal out. Alphonse must be conveyed to the Manor in the carriage which was to be brought up from town. The temperamental French chef would have to be paid extra to put up with the primitive conditions Everhart suspected were to be found in the kitchens. But, even over a campfire, Alphonse could produce a better meal than did Sir Minnow's impertinent Mrs. Gates and so he would tell the Frenchman. Old Mrs. Gates had been Sir Minnow's housekeeper, cook, and general bottle-washer . . . and, although not in recent years perhaps, had very likely provided more personal favors as well. It was quite time to pension the woman off . . . another thing he must add to the growing list of things to do.

In his abstraction, Lord Everhart forgot himself to the point it was necessary he be reminded he was chased. He passed the port decanter to Elliot while wondering when the women had left the dining room. He'd better get his wits together or dear little Cassandra would find him easy prey—especially with Lady Melicent's advice.

An inspiration hit him. Of course! He must find a

moment of privacy and beg little Georgi to protect him from her wicked cousin's wiles! Would the child do it? He remembered her daring in the churchyard—climbing up to scrub off a statue of all things!—and there was that nicely dry sense of humor she'd revealed now and again. Very likely the chit would happily oblige him in his need to foil her cousin. It was just the sort of lark to appeal to a hoyden on the verge of womanhood.

Lord Everhart, having reminded himself of the girl's youth, made a mental note to remember to treat her gently and as the child she was. It wouldn't do to get carried away and begin a serious flirtation with one so young— however appealing her dimples and the twinkle in her eyes. . . .

Once again Lord Everhart came near to forgetting to pass on the port decanter. Lord Tivington wondered what had put his guest into such a brown study—a distraction which he'd tacitly allowed by not pressing conversation on the man. But now he'd have to interrupt. It was time to join the ladies, who were waiting to play cards.

Two

The whist tables were set up while the men drank their port. Everhart decided Lady Melicent must have had a hand in forming the first tables but found it possible to ignore the golden-haired beauty seated to his right.

Much to her horror, Cassandra found herself monopolized by her grandfather, who lectured her gently after every hand as to the mistakes she made, and insisting on her attention, made it impossible for her to insert a single word into the conversation between Lord Everhart and her countrified Aunt Marie. Cassandra was not pleased because her mother would not be pleased. Her mother, she knew, was keeping an eye on the situation from the second table—thereby driving Elliot, her partner, to distraction by muffing play after play.

The evening began badly for Georgi, as well. She partnered her Aunt Anne, who lectured her less gently than Cassandra was lectured, although for fewer mistakes. It was, therefore, a relief when she eventually found herself partnering Lord Everhart. His lordship smiled at her, told her kindly that he knew she'd do very well, and turned to speak to Lord Tivington, who now partnered Lady Melicent.

It was not part of Lord Everhart's plan to set up Lady Melicent's hunting fever by flirting before her eyes with Georgi. He treated the girl as the child he believed her to be. In the churchyard he'd thought she was fifteen at most, but seeing her in an evening gown with her hair up in a simple style, he decided she was just out of the schoolroom, getting on for seventeen, perhaps. Perhaps he'd adjust his plan of using her to fend off her cousin. It wouldn't hurt the child to learn something of the gentle art of flirtation before she was dragged to London and the Marriage Mart as she would be all too soon.

However that might be, now was not the time to begin. Without thinking he covered an error in play which Georgi made, took the trick, and led back. It was taken by Lord Tivington, as Everhart expected. Now if Georgi would take the *next* trick and play another spade . . . she did! "Very well done, partner," he said, pleased with her. "I hoped you'd do that."

"My grandfather taught me the way of it some time ago, my lord," she said, blushing slightly. "I didn't quite understand how it worked, but I saw just how it should go when you played out your cards that way."

"Now, why did I teach her any such a thing? I dislike of all things to lose a bid, but when it's done as smoothly as that, I deserve to be beaten. Well, Melicent? Shall we concede? The tea tray is coming in and Everhart will wish to return home while he has light since there is no moon tonight. I know my poor daughters hoped for another rubber or two. You will indulge them by returning to play again, my lord?" he asked Everhart.

"The Manor is in a sad state, but once I've installed my own cook, and hired servants to clean up the worst of the dirt, perhaps I may invite you there for an evening?"

"Do not stand on ceremony with us, my lord," purred Lady Melicent. "We will look for you whenever you care to drop by."

"Yes. Do feel free," said Lord Tivington, glaring at

his daughter-in-law's presumption in handing out invitations to a home not her own. "I have eaten Mrs. Gates's food, you see, so I know what you suffer. We can always lay another cover at table, my lord, if you find yourself on our side of your property near mealtime. As you must know our borders meet along the stream."

"I haven't determined my boundaries exactly and am not yet certain about my neighbors, but if we border on that stream, then it is to *you* I must speak about that abominable bridge near the mill?"

"And about the mill. Sir Minnow became quite lax the last few years: No direct heir and much illness, you see, so he ceased to care. When the mill fell into disrepair he didn't fix it, and the country people have suffered by its closing."

Lord Everhart gathered up the cards, shuffling them together neatly. "I had always assumed he'd leave the place to Mr. Sedgewycke or Mrs. Compton," he said in an idle tone, but the eyes that met Lord Tivington's had a curious sharpness to them.

"His wife's great-niece and -nephew?" asked his lordship. "He took them in off and on and it was generally believed around the county that they'd inherit, but he once told me property should stay in a family. I think no matter how distant the relationship, he'd have left the estate to someone of his own. You are the great-great-grandson of his great-uncle, are you not?"

"I haven't worked out the exact relationship, my lord, but that sounds about right." Lord Everhart accepted a cup and saucer from Georgi's hands and smiled at her. He caught the soft sound of her indrawn breath and took another look at her. She reddened slightly and turned away to take the last cup to her cousin Elliot. He followed her graceful progress. "Will you excuse me, my lord. I wish to speak with Miss Beverly, if you do not object?"

"Which Miss Beverly?" asked Lord Tivington on a dry note. "There are four of them present this evening."

Everhart grinned in appreciation of his lordship's mildly taunting tone. "It could become confusing, could it not? I refer to Miss Georgi Thomasina . . . Your daughters are interesting, intelligent women, but I find I've little to say to the fourth Miss Beverly." His eyes met his host's, communicating a warning he was not to be trapped into a marriage with the beauty.

"She's a peawit," agreed Lord Tivington. "I say as few words as possible to her myself. But I must have words with both her and her brother and will head them off while you speak to my Georgi." It was Lord Tivington's turn to express a warning. "She is an innocent, my lord. Trusting as a puppy and just as much joy. I would not wish that changed."

"She is, as you say, a delight. I will be careful."

The two men nodded slightly, understanding each other tolerably well. Lord Tivington strolled across the salon, collecting Cassandra, who had her eyes firmly fixed on Lord Everhart and taking her with him to speak with her brother. Neither Elliot nor Cassie enjoyed the next few minutes.

While Lord Tivington lectured the pair, Lord Everhart managed a few words with Georgi. "Child, I wish to ask a favor of you," he said softly, his eye on Lady Melicent, who was quite obviously torn between interfering in his tête-à-tête with Georgi and going to the rescue of her offspring. "I wish to talk to you. Do you ride mornings?"

"Yes. Early. Do you know the mill?"

"About eight?" he suggested

"Or still earlier, please. I must return by nine."

"Tomorrow then. Now I'll take my leave of your delightful aunts and esca—" He chopped off the word and met her eyes when she gurgled, attempting to suppress a chuckle. "I *meant* to say, I've a long drive and there's no moon, so I must leave immediately."

"Of course that is what you meant to say, my lord."

Lord Everhart took a deeper look into her twinkling eyes. She looked older, more mature, somehow. He shook away a tingle of unease. No lady would climb up onto a statue's plinth merely to scrub it off. She must be a child still, and not *possibly* more than fifteen or sixteen. Five minutes later he was gone.

"What did you say?" Lord Everhart yawned as Hamish pulled back another drape. He noted the dust motes floating in the weak sunbeams and added still another job to the list, which grew and grew. This room must be given priority. He'd not sleep another night in such dust and dirt!

"I said, m'lord," Hamish repeated, "that a guest arrived about two of the clock. I'm very much surprised you weren't awakened by the ruckus."

"I heard nothing. The house, despite its many problems, is soundly built. What guest?"

"I understand he is a Mr. Sedgewycke, Sir Minnow's nephew."

"Great-nephew," corrected Everhart. "What is he doing here?"

"I am led to understand from Mrs. Gates's tirades that he comes whenever he is in dun territory. One assumes, if the old besom is correct—but mind, now, I tend to disbelieve every other word she utters—that the young gentleman has, again, found himself in that unenviable condition."

Everhart blinked. "Sir Minnow is dead."

"Quite so, m'lord."

"Sir Minnow is dead and the scapegrace now expects to batten himself on *me?* This is ridiculous. What is the hour?"

"Just on the half hour, m'lord. You did request I wake you after six?"

"Yes. *And* that Alexander be brought around. Have you laid out my riding gear?"

"Yes, m'lord." Hamish approached the bed, holding out Lord Everhart's wildly patterned robe, which looked very much as if it had escaped from an Eastern seraglio. "And what is one to do about Mr. Sedgewycke?"

"He'll have to wait his turn. I'll add him to *The List.*" Half humorously and half peevishly, he suggested, "About twenty items down, don't you think, Hamish?"

Fifteen minutes later Everhart rode toward the old mill. Below it was a bridge which, near as made no mind, seemed about to collapse into the stream. A nicely boned silvery white mare was tethered to a tree not far from it. There was, he knew, a fairly well-maintained ford just about there, obviously used in place of the rickety bridge. His gelding nickered softly and the mare shifted a few paces until she looked toward the approaching rider. Everhart glanced around. Where, he wondered, was Miss Beverly.

Miss Beverly had given him up. Rather morose, she was seated with her bare feet dangling into the slowly moving water of the stream. Her habit was hiked up very nearly to her knees, her elbows holding it in place, and she'd bent forward, sinking her chin into her hands. Everhart looked over the bank at the girl's bent back and felt a strange softening toward her. He wanted her to be the happy, sparkling creature he'd met in the churchyard, and wondered how to go about making her so. Not by informing her he'd caught her in another contretemps, of course. She'd be embarrassed to be found barefoot and wet. It behooved him to back off and make a racket so she could set herself to rights.

He did just that and the next time he approached, she was sitting primly enough, her feet tucked out of sight, although a part of one stocking peeked from beneath the neatly arranged skirts. "Good morning," he called. "How did you get down there?"

She twisted to look up at him. "If you go along a few yards, you'll find a sort of path . . . Yes," she added as he reached the spot. "Just there."

He seated himself on a boulder a few feet away from hers. "There is something very nice about running water, is there not?"

"I think so. This has always been a favorite spot of mine." She threw a pebble into the stream and turned her head. "I'd given you up, my lord, and was about to return home," she said in the frank way he was coming to admire.

"I was delayed by news of unexpected company. A Mr. Sedgewycke arrived during the night . . ." His brows snapped together at Miss Beverly's lightening spirits. "I suppose you know the sprig well?"

"Oh yes. Sedgie's an old playmate, my lord. I never thought to see him again now Sir Minnow is gone."

"Then you would like it if I allow him to remain?" he asked, his hopes of using the chit for his own purposes fading. He couldn't very well carry on a flirtation with her if she hoped for similar attentions from his guest.

"It would be generous of you to do so. Sedgie would appreciate it, I'm certain. It will be difficult for him to move his workshop."

"Move? *Workshop?* "

"He's an inventor."

"What?"

"An inventor. Last I knew he was attempting to invent

a safety lamp for miners but that was some time ago. Do you know the poor miner wears a candle on his head so he may see his work?"

Everhart nodded, but more interested in Sedgewycke, asked, "He *works* here? I was informed he arrives at the Manor when he's in the basket—I mean, in need of a refuge because he's in financial difficulty!"

She chuckled. "I know what it means to be in the basket. I've been very well educated, you see," she explained before adding, "That may be what Mrs. Gates believes, but Sedgie is quite well off and he doesn't need to batten on you." Her eyes twinkled just as Everhart had hoped, but not because of anything he'd done. "Sedgie does the unforgivable, you see: He *works*."

"Just what does he work at?"

"Whenever he can talk an engineer or contractor into taking him on as an assistant he is in his element. I believe he last worked at Taymouth Castle helping the Elliots construct what is said to be a towering Gothic stair hall. I haven't seen it myself, of course, but it was written up with illustrations in one of Grandfather's journals and I have wondered ever since how it was accomplished." She smiled. "Rather impressive, is he not?"

"*You* seem to think so," said Everhart slowly.

"Yes. I once thought he'd make me a proper suitor when I was old enough, but he's become such a fusspot about what a woman should and should not do." Georgi shook her head. "It's such a bore, this attitude men have that a woman must be an empty-headed beauty placed on a pedestal where she is to remain except when doing her lord and master's bidding. So utterly dreary and so ridiculous to think a woman has no thoughts or ambitions . . ."

Something inside Everhart unwound and only then did he realize how tense he'd become. He didn't pause to wonder why, but asked, lightly, "Am I to understand you and Mr. Sedgewycke come to cuffs on this topic?"

His brows were nicely arched and again Georgi noted it with envy. "Yes. On that and many other topics. He can't bear to be contradicted, at least not by a woman. And, except on scientific subjects, he has some very foolish notions. So we argue."

Everhart studied her. She looked back at him, those big oddly colored eyes wide, questioning. "You don't sound as if you were nursing a *tendre* for him," he said cautiously.

Her low-timbred, bubbly laughter sent a shiver up Everhart's spine. That laugh would draw every man who *was* a man into her orbit, hoping to hear it again and again, and to win her so it peeled only for his own personal satisfaction. That is, it would were she a trifle older, he reminded himself. "You said something, Miss Beverly?" he asked, a spot of color reddening his cheeks.

"I only said that my having a *tendre* for Sedgie was the oddest notion. Have you *met* your guest yet?"

"Why no. He was still abed when I left the Manor."

"Let me describe poor Sedgie as I last saw him. He is very tall, my lord. And overly thin. At least, he was three years ago. Grandfather assured me he'll fill out when he gains his full growth but I don't know . . . Anyway, Grandfather says that he is slow to develop his body, since he has, from an early age, been interested only in mental things. Then there is his hair; it already recedes far up his forehead with a silly forelock which dangles in his eyes. That wouldn't be important, of course, if I loved him, but how can one love a man who considers one an irritant or, alternately, his personal slave?" Georgi's brow arched just as her grandfather's did when asking such a question.

"Slave?"

"Yes. Often he needed help in his inventing—holding things and passing him tools and things like that. He discovered I was excellent help because I am interested and calls on me whenever he needs an assistant or *did,* until Aunt Marie said I mustn't. It could be interesting you know, until he'd tell me to"—she deepened her voice—" 'dub your mummer and give me some peace, brat.' "

Another layer of tension Everhart hadn't known he felt lifted. "So you are a brat, are you?"

"Not always," she said demurely.

He gave her a sharp look, but she stared over the water and not up under her lashes in the flirtatious manner he'd expected. "Hmm. And when not a brat, what are you then?"

"Oh, this and that." She looked at him then, but it was a considering look with nothing of the coquette about it. "I don't think I'll tell you. Very likely you'd not approve. How do you go on at the Manor, my lord," she asked, handing him a change of subject.

It didn't work. He simply grinned at her. "None of that . . . brat. I begin to know you, I think. Turning into a properly boring young lady at this point won't work. Miss Beverly, if I were to ask . . ." he said, drawing in a deep breath—and stopped.

"Yes, my lord?"

He stared at her, found that curious, questioning look back in her eyes. He reached out and chucked her lightly under her chin, impelled by something he didn't recognize. "You will very likely mature into a minx, my child. Dear me, do I *dare* ask of you what I'd fully intended asking when I, quite reprehensibly, suggested we meet this morning?"

It appeared to be a rhetorical question so Georgi waited silently. That, too, was unusual in Lord Everhart's experience. Every woman he'd ever met would have been all over him to tell her what he meant, wondering what it was he wanted and making it impossible for him to think or, for that matter, difficult to slip a response into their babble.

"You are a delightful chit, my child. I can understand why your grandfather warned me to be careful with you. I, too, would be sorry to see you change."

"Is that a compliment, my lord?"

"It is."

"If I were standing I'd curtsy. As it is I'll merely say, thank you very much," she said primly.

He grinned. "I'd very much like to see that curtsy, Miss Beverly." He reached over and pulled the stocking from under her skirt, then dangled it over the water. "Your bare toes would make it an interesting exercise, would they not? Now, shall I drop this in or will you pay a forfeit?"

"That depends on the forfeit," she said with that rather dry adult note he'd heard once or twice before.

Again he hesitated. But no. If she were as old as she sometimes seemed, she'd have been presented to the *ton*. "The forfeit . . ." He eyed her, wondering what her reaction would be if he, again, suggested a kiss as he had in the churchyard. "I wish to see the curtsy, of course," he said, squelching such unsuitable notions.

"I think you must drop the stocking, my lord. I do not feel like curtsying."

She meant it! Lord Everhart's brows rose. Laughing, he tossed the bit of apparel into her lap. She bundled it into a ball and stuffed it into her pocket. He suspected she was a trifle more embarrassed than she wished him to know. "Well, brat. I suppose I must either make that request of you or wish you good morning and allow us both to return to breakfast." For another long moment he studied her. "Your cousin."

"Cassandra?"

"Hmm. Are you old enough to understand that there are women who will go to any length to trap a man into marriage?"

She looked at him curiously. "Yes."

He chuckled again. "Just yes? No long explanation? No excuses?"

"No."

This time he saw a twitch to her lips and laughed outright. With that last response she was deliberately baiting him! "*Going* to become a minx? You've already become one! Perhaps I should teach you to respect your elders . . ."

"What of my cousin, my lord," she said, interrupting him.

He allowed the change of subject. "She is one of those women, the sort who will go to any length to marry the man of her choice."

"And you are her choice?"

"I may sound a coxcomb but I believe I am. It is my opinion she has followed me here with no other purpose in mind. She'd not have left the pleasures of Brighton for any other reason."

"My aunt and cousin come every summer, my lord."

"At this time?"

Georgi frowned. "Later, usually . . . Does my aunt have a hand in this?"

"I believe they work together."

"You have no wish to marry Cassie?"

"Good heavens *no.*"

Those curiously questioning eyes studied him yet again. "She's very beautiful."

"And hasn't two thoughts in her head to rattle together."

"Is that important? My Aunt Marie thinks men do not

like women to be intelligent. She is forever scolding me because I disappear into Grandfather's study or the library. She scolds *him* for allowing me to stay there."

"From what I've seen I suspect his lordship *encourages* you to remain."

"That is our secret which, if you please, you will not reveal to my aunt," she said with a combined primness and tartness. "My lord?"

"I'll stand pat and won't stain," he said promptly. "But, about your cousin . . ."

Again he seemed at a loss, so Georgi suggested, "You wish to use me as a stalking horse."

"*Stalking* the lady is the last thing I wish to do, but hiding behind your skirts to escape her ploys? Especially those designed to get me alone? Yes. Will you play up to my teasing of you and not allow her mother, at any time, to catch me alone with her?"

"I will do what I can, my lord," she said slowly.

"That is all I can ask, is it not?"

"But," she objected, "are you *certain* you don't wish to marry Cassie?"

"Very sure. Why are you so insistent on that point?"

"My Aunt Marie insists Cassie is a perfect example of all a man wants in a wife and she has been thrown up to me as an example of all I *should* be for so long, I find it difficult to turn around and accept that it is not so."

"Your cousin has been out for several years. If she were all a man wished in a bride, then she would have been married long ago."

"Do you think so?" Georgi brightened, then shook her head. "But no, that cannot be right. She *has* had offers."

"But none of the sort she wishes. None which would raise her to a position she believes should be hers."

"Hmm. Yes. At least, which *Aunt Melicent* would approve."

He caught her sidelong glance and asked, "What now, brat?"

"I've difficulty believing my cousin would settle so firmly on a particular man, having received no particular encouragement on the man's part."

Lord Everhart colored, feeling the heat begin at his ears and flow throughout his face. "Well . . . yes. You see . . ."

"Yes, my lord?"

"You have too much nous, Miss Beverly, and have caught me out for a peep-o-day boy. I must explain although it does me no credit. I believed your cousin to be much more up to snuff than she is . . ." His brows snapped together. ". . . than I was *led* to believe," he corrected himself. "I overheard her own mother say . . . Blast! They *planned* it." He groaned.

"My lord?"

"An old trick. I was to be caught making delicious love to your cousin and forced to ask for her hand. One kiss, however, and I realized she was *not* experienced, was *not* the wanton I'd been led to believe, so, fortunately, I saw through the plan in time to escape from her mother's 'discovery' of us. I picked her up bodily and moved to where other couples were strolling."

"My cousin made no complaint?"

"I believe my expression of disgust may have intimidated her into holding her tongue. But it hasn't, I see, given *her* a disgust of *me*. So, will you be my shield, maiden?" he asked wistfully.

"Do you wish an Amazon or a Valkyrie, my lord?"

He hid his surprise that she knew of either.

Thoughtfully, Georgi added, "I don't care to mutilate myself as the Amazons were said to do—"

His brows rose at her reference to the fact the warrior women removed their right breast so it would not interfere with their bowstrings.

"—but neither do I care to guide those slain in battle to Valhalla. You set me a hard choice, my lord."

"I believe *you* suggested there was a choice, brat." She smiled but made no comment. "Perhaps," he continued, "what I wish is not a shield maiden but an esquire. Esquiress?"

"Ah. A shield *bearer* rather than a shield *maid*. I am to attend you when you go into battle, is that it, Sir Knight?"

"It is true I look on your cousin and her mother as the enemy with whom I must do battle and aiding his knight was the portion of an esquire in olden days. Will you?"

She tipped her head and stared across the water. "I wonder if it is disloyal to my family to do so . . . ?"

"What would your most estimable grandfather say? Would he think it proper to punish me by leg-shackling me to that widgeon?"

"Grandfather?" That husky chuckle he loved rippled out again. "Oh, Grandfather dislikes Aunt Melicent and thinks Cassie every bit the nitwit you think her. I believe he'd approve my saving you from their machinations."

"Then we have a deal, brat?"

She wrinkled her nose. "We have a deal on one condition, my lord."

It was his turn to look a trifle wary. "And that is?"

"That you cease calling me brat!"

Three

Hamish quietly entered the breakfast room later that morning as Lord Everhart stoically downed a nearly inedible breakfast. He cleared his throat.

"Yes?" asked Everhart, perfectly willing to be distracted from what could be endured no longer. "Are we making progress?"

"I've hired six women from the village, m'lord, and set them to cleaning your bedroom. They'll proceed to the kitchens in the hopes that, if they are clean, that'll be one thing less about which Alphonse will kick up a dust. I've sent the message concerning the forwarding of the Frenchie himself and the carriages and horses you require. *Mrs. Gates is not pleased,*" he said, finishing his report with a certain severity.

Everhart grimaced. "Mrs. Gates may take her pleasure elsewhere then."

"May I tell her so?" asked Hamish politely.

The grimace changed to a grin. "No, you may not. My elderly relative was remiss in not leaving her an annuity in his will. Whatever we think of her, she gave long years of service and loyalty and must not be turned off for being a trifle queer in the attic now she's reached her dotage."

Hamish sighed. "She too has expressed surprise there was nothing for her." His eyes twinkled slightly, his temper restored. "She mutters, you know, and one feels sorry for the old biddy . . . except when she is shrewing at one." Hamish tipped his head. "Perhaps, m'lord, if it were intimated to her you will see to her future . . . ?"

"Drop her a hint but no more. I've not yet decided just what to do. I'll ask the vicar, Hamish. Vicars have a way of knowing the sort of information I need. Has she relatives, or is there an empty cottage she might have . . . that sort of thing."

"Certainly, m'lord." Hamish cleared his throat. "There is one more problem which I feel must be discussed."

Everhart leaned back in his chair, a mug of ale held in both hands. The ale, he'd decided, was the only decent viand on the table. "Have we not covered the immediate situation?"

"You have a house guest . . ."

"I'd forgotten. Very right of you to bring it to my attention. Can you enlighten me further and tell me where my *guest* might be found?" Everhart fondled the dark silky side of the old pewter tankard. He raised his gaze to meet that of his longtime servant. "You have yet to explain why he was allowed entry last night."

Hamish raised his gaze toward heaven. "He wasn't allowed. He has a key to the side door and had installed his luggage, such as it is, in his usual room before anyone was aware of his arrival. If he'd not dropped a box full of nasty smelly stuff which clattered halfway down the side stairs no one would have known until he appeared at breakfast this morning. He had bread and cheese, m'lord, with his ale and informed me it was the only possible thing to eat in the house. He lives on bread and cold meat or cheese when visiting. He says it is very nearly the only food Mrs. Gates can't ruin."

"Not a total nodcock." Everhart's lips pursed. "What did you think of him?"

Again master's gaze met man's. In their travels, which had been restricted far more than either liked by the seemingly perpetual war with France, they'd come to rely on each other's judgment. Now Hamish too pursed his lips, a thoughtful expression on his long face. "A nicely set-up man. Only enough town bronze to make him acceptable, but he wouldn't have more than that, would he? Not being on the town, I mean. Not a nodcock and no basket scrambler neither. But . . ." Hamish shook his head. "I can't quite put my finger on it, m'lord. Although he's educated and nicely spoken, he . . . Well, he . . ." Again he shook his head. "I just don't know what I think."

After mulling over Hamish's unfinished thoughts, Everhart asked, "Why is he here? Did he say?"

Hamish blinked. *"That's* it, m'lord. That's what's bothered me. He appeared quite at home and unworried he might not be welcome. It didn't seem to occur to him that, now his uncle was dead, things might've changed?"

"Not a clever ploy to batten on me, you think?"

"I think not. But, this evening you may see for yourself . . . assuming you don't want him put off the property before then?" Everhart indicated he wasn't prepared to go to such extremes before he'd even met the man. "Mr. Sedgewycke said he'd be in for dinner if he didn't find himself in the midst of a mess just then and added that, if Mrs. Gates could be coaxed into making it, her mulligatawny soup was usually very nearly edible."

"Then she must be coaxed into making it—which is another job I'll leave to you. What's more, I'll have bread and ham for a luncheon and will eat it at my desk. You have not yet said where my unusual house guest has taken himself off to."

"I didn't think to ask and he didn't say. He did lug

away that box of smelly stuff, however, and left by way of the side door. If you wish to seek him out, I presume there must be an outbuilding to which he took it."

"I wish I *might* take the time to track him down, but there is yet more paper to dig through in the library and several *years* worth of thoroughly confused records in the room Mrs. Gates calls the office." Everhart sighed. "I wonder why I thought it might be interesting to settle this estate myself?"

"You *didn't* think it would be interesting," responded Hamish promptly. "You thought it a long way from Brighton."

The two men grinned. "How well you know me, Hamish."

In the gardens at Beverly Place Miss Cassandra Beverly dawdled her way along the paths, occasionally pointing to a flower which a long-suffering undergardener snipped and laid into the basket he carried over his arm. Miss Cassandra was bored. She had every expectation of remaining bored for so long as her mother insisted they remain at the Place.

Why it was imperative she capture Lord Everhart before he returned to town for the Little Season was a mystery Cassie had yet to solve. She didn't *wish* to marry Lord Everhart. In fact, she was in no particular hurry to give up the pleasures of being a London toast, an incomparable surrounded by suitors and enjoying all the advantages of the annual social scene—unless a miracle happened and one particular man would admit she was alive, that is.

Cassie pouted. It was a look which had led more than one young man to steal a kiss, telling her her lips were delightfully bee-stung and irresistible and it was her fault for being so beautiful that they forgot themselves. She sighed. She'd rather liked those gentle kisses which were given by young men very nearly as inexperienced as she was herself. She *hadn't* enjoyed Lord Everhart's demanding lips.

Her mother said she'd enjoy being a countess and having a huge dress allowance and several houses, but refused to discuss the responsibilities she'd come into. She'd be required to run the earl's houses, plan his parties, and play hostess. It would be her duty to see that the plainest of girls were introduced to the exciting young men who now clustered around her own precious person. It did not seem to Cassie that being a countess and having precedence over her own mother was compensation for all she must give up.

"What's wrong, cousin," called Georgi from the bower, where she'd hidden herself away with a book detailing Marco Polo's travels.

Cassandra dismissed the gardener and wandered over to the vine-covered nook. She dropped gracefully into the cast-iron chair across from where her cousin reclined on a lounge.

"You are very lucky, Georgi." She pouted.

"I am?" asked Georgi cautiously.

"Hmm. Here you are with no one telling you whom you must marry or forever pushing you to do exactly what you don't wish to do and Grandfather giving you anything you want whenever you want it and allowing you too much freedom and letting you grow up a hoyden which I think must be quite a lot of fun except it's quite likely to make you a byword in the *ton* which would be insupportable, of course." She gasped for breath. "It really isn't fair."

"You have it wrong if you think Grandfather gives me much of anything."

"But you have your horse and all the books you wish," pointed out Cassie. "For myself, of course, I'd ask for jewels and to go to London every Season and . . ." The sigh was extreme. "I don't know. Perhaps my very own phaeton lined in gold which would set off my gowns and I'd have my footmen in uniforms to match and a team of that pale golden color one sees occasionally and . . ." Again her voice trailed off. "Georgi, how do you stand it? I mean, living here all the year-round and never going anywhere and never seeing anyone special and . . ." A single tear ran down the peaches-and-cream cheek. Another followed.

Georgi marveled: It was a mystery how her cousin could cry and only look more beautiful. How could Lord Everhart not fall in love with her?

"You don't say anything," said Cassandra. "You have no conversation, do you, Georgi?"

"None which would interest you, I fear." When there was no response, she asked, "Why are you so sad? I know you don't really care to visit here each year, but I don't recall that you've cried about it."

"You don't understand."

"No and I won't, will I, unless you explain?" She waited. "Cassie, I truly think you must tell me." There was a still deeper sigh, which, Georgi noticed, did interesting things to her cousin's bosom. Would she had a decent bosom, one which did interesting things when one sighed! "Don't be tiresome, Cassie," she insisted a bit crossly. "Do explain. Who knows? Perhaps I may help you."

"I don't think anyone can help, but it's really very simple. You see, I must charm Lord Everhart and wring an offer from him. At once. My mother says it is beyond everything great that he decided to come to the Manor this summer. There will be, she says, no competition;

not that I've competition even in London, of course. I am a great beauty, you know."

This was said with such simplicity Georgi laughed. She received a look of suspicion in return. "Now, don't take a pet, Cassie. I know very well you are the beauty of the family. In fact I've never seen anyone more beautiful."

"Yes," objected the beauty, "but his lordship doesn't seem to notice it. I don't understand it."

"His lordship? You refer to Lord Everhart?"

"Yes. He was quite attentive for a time last Season and Mama quite got her hopes up, but then it didn't come to anything and he ceased paying me any particular attentions. It was most embarrassing."

Georgi was growing immune to the effect a deep sigh had on her cousin's figure.

"Mother says I must enrapture him again, but I don't know that I want to."

Georgi, who had awakened from a very interesting dream involving his lordship only that morning, blinked. How could her cousin not want to? "Why?" she asked bluntly.

A faint flush rushed into her cousin's cheeks, improving her already incomparable looks. Her eyes flickered from side to side. "I don't wish to discuss it. Certainly not with a girl who hasn't had a Season. You wouldn't understand, Georgi."

"He kissed you."

Cassie's eyes widened. "How did you know?"

Georgi ignored the question. Cassie was often surprised at what Georgi knew because she didn't understand the simple operation of adding two and two. Not that adding was necessary here. Georgi had Everhart's confession on which to base her statement. She asked, "You didn't like his kisses?"

The beautiful girl shuddered, grimaced, and came as

near as Georgi had ever seen to losing her looks. "It was *awful*. It was like a huge bear mauling one about. Why, he actually disarranged my hair, Georgi! I didn't think it would be like that at all. Kissing, I mean." She pouted. "Well, it isn't. Not always. I *know*."

"You'd been kissed before?"

"Hmm. More than once. And it wasn't rough and nasty. It was quite pleasant, actually."

A boy's kiss, thought Georgi. 'So you don't want him to kiss you?'

"No. But Mama says I mustn't be missish. She says women must accept such from their husbands even when we don't like it and even when they forget themselves and disarrange one's hair or gown. She says some men do forget themselves and I told her I'd much rather marry one who did not but she says the earl is by far the most eligible suitor at hand and I must just put up with it."

Georgi studied her cousin. How could anyone be so far under another's control that they hadn't a thought in their head but what had been put there. "If you really don't wish to marry the earl, then you should tell Grandfather. He'll not have you forced into a marriage you don't at all aspire to."

"Grandfather?" Cassie looked doubtful, then shook her head. "Oh no, Georgi. He indulges you to a shocking degree . . ."

One of those thoughts, thought Georgi cynically.

". . . but he never indulges me. He doesn't like me. He doesn't even think I'm pretty," she finished as if that somehow clinched her argument.

"He thinks you pretty, Cassie. And you are wrong he'd not make a push to stop a wedding you'd no wish to enter into. Would you like me to ask him? For you?"

"No. Oh no, Georgi. You don't understand. Mama would . . . would . . . oh dear."

Georgi interrupted. "Your father then. Surely my uncle would not wish you unhappy."

Cassie looked blank for a moment, her lips slightly parted. "Papa?" she asked as if she had to think who that might be. She closed her mouth and shook her head. "No, no. It is *Mama* who rules the roost." An expression of panic crossed her lovely features. "It is *Mama* who . . . Georgi, Mama would . . . would . . ." Unable to complete her thought, Cassie wrung her hands.

Georgi tipped her head to one side. She'd read of the action, a common if useless behavior for the heroines in novels when finding themselves in some Gothic situation, but this was the first time she'd observed it in life. What was more, Cassie looked truly frightened.

"You *mustn't*, Georgi," said Cassie earnestly. "Mama would be so *angry*. I could not bear it. I'm not brave like you. She'd make me miserable and she might say I can't go to London again and I'd never have any more pretty gowns or go to balls . . ." Cassie shook her head. "I would die, Georgi. Truly I would."

"But why do you think you'd not be allowed to have another Season?"

"I don't know what music has to do with it, but I believe the dibs, whatever they are, are out of tune."

Georgi knew very well what was meant and it had nothing to do with music. "Your father is in dun territory? I don't believe it."

"It's something Elliot did. Something about cents-percents. I don't understand that either."

Again Georgi did. She wondered if her grandfather knew and thought not since he'd complained at breakfast of Elliot's "decision" to remain for a visit. Very obviously it had been his parents' decision and he'd only pretended, in order to save his pride, that he wished a repairing lease.

"I'm to marry the earl so that all may be well again."

"Settlements."

"Yes. That's what mother said. Settlements. I don't understand about settlements, either."

"It seems to me you don't understand very much at all."

"I don't suppose I do. I'm not expected to, am I? My governess taught me everything I'd need to be a proper young lady and find myself a husband."

"Did she teach you it was proper to let men kiss you?" asked Georgi.

Cassie giggled. "Oh no. She'd say it was exceedingly *improper,* but I've discovered a great deal of Life is not *exactly* as one is taught in the schoolroom. I've been out three years, you know." She frowned.

The frown did not detract from Cassie's beauty. Her cousin was a finished piece of perfection indeed! It was Georgi's turn to sigh. She did so softly.

"And that's another thing," said Cassie, the frown still in place. "It was quite all right to have a second Season. That is permissible. After all, one is very young the first year and quite the innocent and one should not allow one's feelings to lead one astray for fear one might give one's hand to a fortune hunter or a basket scrambler or one of the peep-o-day boys . . ."

Georgi wondered just what fortune hunter had come so close to leading Cassie astray that her mother had told her such a thing.

". . . so a second Season is acceptable. Even a third. But that is enough. I've had my third and am yet unwed. It is most disturbing." The last was said in a toneless voice which led Georgi to believe her cousin was still quoting her mother. "Mama says . . ."

Georgi was not to hear what Mama said. At that moment Elliot poked his head into the bower. "So here is where you hide yourself. You, Georgi, are an abominable hostess. You *should,* you know, make a push to entertain us."

He said his piece in such a prudish, pokered-up tone Georgi wished she could *land him a facer* and *draw his claret* as she had when they were all much younger. Even after all these years there was great satisfaction in recollecting that delightful occasion. His nose had bled so nicely. Even though she'd been sent to bed by Aunt Anne with no supper it had been worth it. Aunt Anne had been outraged by her unladylike behavior, but Grandfather, who had seen the whole, had not. His eyes had twinkled in that nice way they had, and later, he'd come to her bedroom with a tray, telling her she'd displayed to advantage and asking where she'd learned her science. She'd admitted one of the stable lads had taught her how to double up her fist properly with the thumb outside and how to hit out from the shoulder.

"It is not a bad thing for you to know, Georgi," Grandfather had said. "It is never an impossibility that a young lady may be drawn into a situation where she needs to defend herself. However that may be, I must ask you not to fight with your cousin. He is not up to your weight, Georgi. I'd have thought you'd have known it is most ungentlemanly to fight when your opponent has no chance at all." He studied her. "Since this has come to my attention, Georgi, I will, once your cousins have returned home, teach you another trick. Women are at a grave disadvantage with men. Men are so much stronger, you see. I will show you a way which, if you can manage it, will bring down the biggest of them."

Mystified, Georgi had agreed to remind him. She'd not forgotten and now, remembering what she'd been taught, blushed.

"I'm very sorry," said Elliot, not sorry at all, "if my

little lecture has embarrassed you, but you are such a rustic *someone* needs bring you to an understanding of your duty." When she laughed, he added, "It is your duty to entertain guests."

"But you are family, Elliot, and one can't consider you a guest in the usual sense of the word so I don't believe it is my duty. But, if you like, I will ask Grandfather and abide by his decision."

Her cousin blenched. "No, no. Don't bother the old gentleman. Wouldn't wish to put him out by having him discover another of your faults." He grimaced and poked his cane at a wide place between the flags flooring the bower. "Perhaps I'll take a ride into the village."

"Did you bring your hack?" asked Georgi sharply.

"Of course!" Elliot's outrage was quite real this time. "After my last stay here when I was forbidden a mount do you think I'd come without one?"

"Well, see you don't lame him, because you'll not be allowed one of ours to replace him."

"You are an impertinent chit and I've half a mind to tell your chaperones how you go on."

"You'll catch cold at that, Elliot. They may not be great riders themselves, but they have respect for good horseflesh and were quite as shocked as anyone else at the way you treated my mare."

Elliot drew himself up. "An animal which will not obey the reins must be trained to do so."

"I've never had the least trouble with her." Georgi was becoming more incensed by the moment. "Perhaps it was not the fault of the mare but of the rider?"

"I may not be a nonpareil but I'm an excellent rider. I hunt with the Brocklesby Hunt in Lincolnshire, you know."

"Hmm. And override the hounds on all occasions. Or so I've heard."

"Once!" Elliot's ears reddened. "It was an accident. They veered and I didn't notice. I was *not* at fault."

"You never *are* at fault, are you? At least, in your own opinion." Georgi tipped her head. "Elliot, explain to me how it is you are incapable of admitting when you are in the wrong? I have never understood how one cannot take responsibility for one's actions, but you've turned the philosophy of *irresponsibility* into a science. Please explain. I truly don't see how you can stomach blaming the innocent for something which is your fault."

"You become offensive. I will not be in for luncheon, so give my excuses to my aunts. Cassie," he added, glaring at his sister, "don't let our cousin lead you astray. You know how much we count on you."

"Do I?" Elliot actually growled and Cassie cringed. "Oh, yes, Elliot, *of course* I know." He nodded, satisfied, and strolled off.

"Do you always let him bully you that way?" asked Georgi.

"He *pinches*. Once I couldn't wear my newest gown because he left a bruise and the dress revealed the black-and-blue mark. I don't want him to pinch me, Georgi."

"Does you mother know what he does?"

"Of course not. He threatened to pinch me all over if I told anyone." She looked a trifle self-conscious. "Oh dear. I shouldn't have mentioned it to *you*, should I? You must promise you'll not tell. Promise!" she insisted when Georgi hesitated.

"I promise not to tell your mother your brother pinches you," said Georgi slowly.

"Thank you. I'm a little afraid of Elliot, you know."

"Which allows him to be as mean as he pleases. That is the way with bullies. They are only nasty to those who won't fight back."

"Oh, I *couldn't*."

Georgi started to argue but decided to give up trying to put a little backbone into her cousin. It was, she thought, an impossible job and she had other, more important questions. "Cassie, have you never met a man you wished to marry?"

The impossibly big blue eyes wavered, looked down at tightly clenched hands. "Man? Marry?" She grew a trifle pale.

"In three years on the *ton* you've never fallen in love?"

"Love?" If anything Cassie's pale cheeks whitened still more. "Oh, Georgi, you must know it isn't proper to think of *that*. In our station one doesn't *fall in love*. It isn't done. Only the lower orders are so . . . so imprudent."

"But you did, didn't you?" asked Georgi shrewdly. "Who was the man, Cassie?"

Blue eyes rose to meet brown-green eyes. What she read there must have satisfied Cassie that her cousin only asked out of kindness. "You won't tell?" she whispered.

"Tell your mother? Cassie, you *know* I'd not snitch to your mother." That she'd very likely have a long conversation with their grandfather was something Georgi hoped would not occur to her beautiful cousin. It wasn't quite honorable to lead her on this way, but something had to be done or Cassie would be forced into a situation that would ruin her whole life. It wasn't right.

"You'll think I'm silly."

"If I do, I won't laugh," Georgi promised. "Who is he?"

"Oh dear. I don't think I should tell you. I only see him once in a while. He doesn't spend much time in London. Not even in the Season, but he's so handsome and he's kind to me, Georgi, and I like him so very much."

"Does he like you?"

Cassie looked a trifle doubtful. "I don't know. He can't *dislike* me for he *stands up with me* at balls and he *almost never dances.*"

"But what's his name? Not that I'm likely to know him."

"But, you *do.*"

"I do?"

"Yes. It's Mr. Sedgewycke, Georgi. You remember Mr. Sedgewycke, don't you? Georgi?"

"Sedgie?" She stared at her blushing cousin. "I haven't seen him for several years. Not since Aunt Anne forbade me to go over to the Manor and help him like I used to do. She stopped inviting him here, too, which I always thought rather mean of her. But, Cassie, are you sure you love Sedgie? I mean he's not at all like the man I thought you'd fall in love with."

"Why not? He's so tall and so handsome and has perfect features. And there is something about the way that strand of hair in the middle of his scalp falls onto his forehead which makes me want to reach up and push it back and . . ."

"Sedgie?"

"Georgi, you are not at all polite. You are not supposed to look as if you don't believe a word I say to you. It isn't *nice.*"

"The last time I saw Sedgie he was indeed tall, but for the rest of it, I can't believe he's changed so much."

"He's beautiful."

Georgi chuckled. "I can't believe it. Where do you meet him, Cassie?"

"When he's in town he's invited everywhere. Mama explained to me how a hostess invites presentable men to fill in at dinner and stand up at balls. She doesn't know I've a *tendre* for him. You mustn't tell. Georgi. Promise!"

"What a lot of promises you require. He actually goes to *tonish* parties?" Her mind filled with a picture of Sedgie as she'd last seen him, Georgi chuckled. "I wonder what he finds to talk about?"

"I don't wish to mislead you, Georgi. He doesn't go to *many* parties. But he is well connected and he obliges ladies who are related to him. Except his sister." Cassie giggled. "He says his sister is a widgeon and a pinchpenny and he won't have a thing to do with her."

"You refer to Alicia Compton?"

"Has he another sister?"

"Not that I know of. I don't know her well, but she came most summers to stay with Sir Minnow. I've heard she did so because she hates to spend a pence. Perhaps it isn't that she's a pinchpenny, Cassie, but that she's in straightened circumstances."

"Oh no, it can't be that. She's called the Golden Widow, you know, even though she's dark as a Gypsy. It's her money they mean, you see. Mr. Compton was *very* well to do. A cit, of course, but he left her everything and she's pursued by all the fortune hunters, but will have nothing to do with them. Some of them are quite handsome, too."

"Cassie, you wouldn't wish to be married just for your money, even by a very handsome man."

"Nooo," said her cousin doubtfully. "But it isn't likely, is it? It is I who must marry for money."

Cassie sighed again and again it did that interesting thing to her bosom. Did she know? Georgi was tempted to ask, but restrained her curiosity, not wishing to put Cassie to the blush. Blushing would only do delightful things to Cassie' s complexion. It really wasn't fair, thought Georgi. Besides, something was bothering her. She'd told Lord Everhart she'd help protect him from her aunts' plots. But if her uncle was in dun territory, didn't family loyalty require her to help him recoup his fortune in whatever why he could? Even if that meant sacrificing poor Cassie? *Bah,* thought Georgi. Cassie wasn't a bad girl and didn't deserve to suffer because her brother was one of those peep-o-day boys against whom young girls were warned!

This mental argument was interrupted by a mild twinge in the region of Georgi's stomach. She lifted the watch she'd pinned to the bodice of a comfortable old gown. "It is very nearly time for Booth to lay a cold collation in the dining room. I'm surprised how sharp set I am since I've done so little this morning. Shall we return to the house and smarten ourselves up a trifle and join the family?"

Cassie lifted her hands to touch her hair. "Am I *very* windblown, Georgi? Oh, yes, do let us go in *at once.* I so dislike it when I am not *point de vice.* It is so very important to always look one's absolute best," she finished in a confiding tone.

It seemed to pass right by Cassie that Georgi had dressed by guess when she'd changed from her riding habit after her ride. Her gown was a faded old thing she loved for its comfort and loose fit. Her hair was pulled back and tied off with an unpressed ribbon which didn't match, and the hat she'd put on—knowing her Aunt Marie would scold if she was discovered without one— had a broken brim and no trim. Picturing how far from *point de vice* she must look, Georgi broke into chuckles. Cassie joined her, but obviously had not the least notion why they were laughing. Later, thought Georgi, she must remember to describe the scene to Grandfather. He'd enjoy the irony, as well.

Grandfather didn't come to luncheon and it was some time before Georgi found herself free to go to him. Aunt Marie enforced the rule that Georgi practice on the pianoforte for an hour after lunch and then suffer another half hour working on some bit of handiwork. Grandfather refused to interfere to any great extent in his daughters' views of his granddaughter's upbringing, but he had taken pity on her to the extent he said a half hour a day with her hated needle would be quite sufficient.

Finished for that day with the bit of embroidery she was currently mangling, Georgi found Lord Tivington in his study, but quite willing to set aside his book when she asked if he had a moment because a few things were worrying her and she thought he should know part of it and might help with the rest.

"Something my intrepid Georgi cannot handle?"

"I can do nothing about the fact Elliot seems to have come so close to ruining his father that the family is determined to see Cassie married for the largest possible settlement."

"I think you'd better start at the beginning and tell me what you've managed to dig out of your artless little cousin."

"She is easy to manipulate, is she not? I suppose I shouldn't do it, but she confided a bit by accident and I felt I should discover what she meant." Georgi explained about the cents-percents and that her uncle must have been badly strained financially if her aunt was determined Cassie wed Everhart at once. She went on about Elliot's bullying ways and Cassie's fear of her brother. Georgi decided it would be ungentlemanly to reveal Cassie's secret love so didn't tell about it, although she did mention that Cassie was not enthralled with the notion of marrying the earl.

"They had a . . . misunderstanding . . . one evening

during the Season," she explained vaguely. Between Everhart's revelation and Cassie's admission, she knew, in some detail, what it *was,* but again she couldn't see any reason her grandfather need know *why* Cassie had taken his lordship in disgust.

Lord Tivington's eyes narrowed thoughtfully. "So George Elliot is more of a loose screw than I'd believed. There is little I can do about that, Georgi. If my son and heir is too proud to admit to me he is in difficulties I cannot help him directly."

"You will allow Everhart to be trapped by my aunt if she can manage it?"

Sharp old eyes flew to her face. "Trapped?"

Georgi flushed, but she met her grandfather's gaze. "Something I was told makes me believe Cassie has already been used once as bait in a trap. My aunt's quarry managed to slip out of the noose before it could close. I should not have mentioned it."

"You believe there to have been a deliberate plot?"

"I do."

"I do not approve."

"Nor do I, which is one reason I've approached you. The other is that, if my uncle is truly under the hatches—and please don't scold that I'm using cant because I don't know enough about finances, despite your tutoring, to know the proper term . . ." She paused, blinked, frowned. "Where was I?"

"You were suggesting that if my son is under the hatches, then . . . what?"

"Oh. Well, even if he *is,* I do not think his pride should force him to sacrifice his daughter. It is not fair to Cassie."

"Arranged marriages are not uncommon, Georgi. A financial or dynastical reason is often sufficient basis for a marriage contract."

Georgi sighed. "I see I've not had enough practice to be a good conspirator. I am forced to reveal something I'd rather not."

"Did you promise not to?"

"Only that I'd not tell her mother! I'm not *that* bad a conspirator. The fact is that Cassie has given her heart but feels it is hopeless."

"And is it?"

"Perhaps under the present circumstances it is. I mean, I believe the man is very likely in need of a dowry, but I do not think it need be a fortune. I don't really know very much about his situation, now I think about it. But that's my impression."

"The present circumstances to which you refer is the need for a settlement?"

"Yes."

"Hmm."

"Grandfather, even if she were *not* in love, I think it wrong *she* be made to suffer—and I think she *would*—for her brother's faults."

"You needn't put on such a stern face, Georgi. I am in agreement on that point. My grandson should be made, for once, to face the consequences of his outrageous behavior." Her grandfather's expression lightened and his eyes twinkled. "In fact, Georgi, what do you say to the notion that it is *he* who be made to marry? We must find him an *heiress!*"

"That would be poetic justice, but an appropriate heiress does not grow on . . ." Georgi fell silent, her eyes slowly widening as she stared at nothing in particular. She brought her eyes back into focus and her gaze met her grandfather's interested look. "The Golden Widow."

"The who? Or do I mean whom?" he asked politely.

"You mean who, I think. But *I* mean Mrs. Compton. If Cassie is to be believed, the woman's not down to her last few pence as I've always thought, but inherited an obscenely large fortune from that cit she married. She is, however, considered parsimonious and unwilling to spend a groat." Georgi grinned. "That, I am led to understand, is the reason she battened herself on her Sir Minnow each summer. He'd give her free room and board."

"If what you say is true, then Mrs. Compton might have been the answer to a prayer, but she cannot, er, *batten* herself on Lord Everhart, can she?"

"Can she not? Her brother has!"

"What?"

"Sedgie has come again this summer just as usual."

"How did you discover that?"

Georgi waved a hand in an airy fashion, knowing full well she would not fool her grandfather for an instant. "Country news travels fast."

Her grandfather noticed she did not quite meet his eyes, but he let it pass. "You think Mrs. Compton, too, will show her face?"

"I think so. Can you," she asked rather diffidently, "suggest that Lord Everhart allow her to stay? If she comes, that is?"

"How can I do any such thing? It would be most improper."

"I was afraid you'd say that. I suppose I must do it myself."

"You saw him this morning."

It was not a question and once again Georgi was startled by her grandfather's omniscience. She said, "Well yes. I rode out as usual and . . ."

"You are going to tell a fib. I always know, Georgi."

She pouted, scowled, and clenched her fists in frustration. "And you always refuse to explain how you know. It is unfair, my lord Grandfather!"

"I refuse again: With you, child, I need every advantage I can get. Now tell me the whole of it."

She sighed. "Last night we made an assignation to meet near the mill."

Lord Tivington frowned. "I warned you against the man, Georgi."

"He isn't interested in setting me up as his latest flirt, if that concerns you."

She chuckled, but to his lordship's ears the laugh had a faintly watery sound which he disliked hearing.

"I believe," she said, "that he thinks me still in the schoolroom, Grandfather. He calls me brat and other equally derogatory things. Lord Everhart, far from making the least push to turn me up sweet, has asked me to place myself as a buffer between himself and Cassie. I said I would, but I'm torn, wondering if I should allow things to take their natural course. Even if Cassie thinks herself in love with another I suspect Lord Everhart has enough address to overcome that. If he wishes to. Which he *would* if he were engaged to her."

"If he were *forced* to become engaged to that nitwit, he would very likely drown himself rather than make up to her!"

"Grandfather!"

"I've listened to you very patiently, Georgi. I've told you I do not think Cassie should be forced into a marriage that is repugnant to her—but I think marriage to a man with no money and no social standing would be wrong for the chit: She is one of nature's butterflies, my dear, and there is really no place for such as she, except to flutter around in society. I don't, however, see why *Everhart* should be forced to keep her there."

"Then I should carry out my part in protecting his lordship?"

"I think you must, my dear. But, Georgi, you will be

careful, will you not? He is a charming rogue and I would not like your heart bruised."

"So long as he thinks me practically in the nursery he'll not treat me as a woman and surely one does not lose one's heart when one is being scolded and teased and generally treated as one of the infantry. I will not disabuse him of his misconception if you prefer that I not."

Again Lord Tivington was a trifle worried—this time by the touch of wistfulness he heard in his granddaughter's voice. "I hope I'll not regret inviting the man into our home!"

"He'll soon finish at the Manor and be gone. There is little likelihood he'll be here long enough to discover my age." There was a pause. "If that is all, we've several hours before we must dress for dinner. I think I may be able to complete the next chapter in my new story."

"Granddaughter," laughed Lord Tivington, "I do believe you're growing up. That was a very tactful way of telling me you've had enough of my lecturing and wish to be excused!"

"Is that what I did?" she asked demurely.

"Minx!"

She laughed and moved to the desk in the large window embrasure. She pulled off the chain she wore around her neck and used the key dangling from it to unlock the drawers. Very soon she was absorbed in her writing.

Her grandfather watched her with a fond eye, wondering what sort of tale she was weaving this time and very interested in reading it but knowing he'd not see a word until she'd polished it to her satisfaction. When it was ready to send to the publisher who had bought her preceding two books *then* he'd be allowed to read it. Lord Tivington was quite proud of Georgi's story-telling ability. It was really too bad, he thought, that the world looked down on women who showed talent.

The old man's eyes narrowed. It would not be easy, he feared, to find the sort of man his granddaughter had recently described as acceptable to her as a husband, but finding him was necessary. Much as he hated to admit it, Georgi *was* of an age to marry. Worse, *he* was of an age when he might not have much time to see to her future. Another sigh drifted into the summer air that day. This one was that of an elderly gentleman who saw an end to one of his more selfish indulgences, the keeping of his favorite granddaughter by his side.

Four

Three straight hours were enough when sorting letters from accounts due and accounts paid and both from a myriad of odd bits of paper on which Sir Minnow had written lists reminding himself of what he must do and when he must do it. Very occasionally a line would be neatly crossed through, but most often the same items appeared on one list after another. Sir Minnow seemed to have planned much and carried through little during the last years of his life.

There was much more of the same, but Everhart felt virtuous and deserving of a rest, so—with difficulty—he opened the double doors leading out onto the cracked and weedy terrace beyond. Three hours and so little progress, he marveled, and decided his solicitor's stipend and his agent's wages should be raised. If they, regularly, put up with a fraction of the work that still awaited him, then they deserved more than they were currently getting—whatever that might be!

Everhart started down the broad steps to the garden below. One wobbled. His lordship scribbled a reminder it be fixed in the little booklet he'd found for the purpose. There was so much already on The List he wondered if Hamish knew where to begin. Hamish, however, reveled in complications, so he was unlikely to be daunted.

If it were left up to him, Everhart thought, most likely he would take himself to a local solicitor and put the Manor up for sale just to rid himself of the problems. But that would be cutting off his nose to spite his face: He liked the Cotswolds. As a member of the Berkeley Hunt, he came every year for the fox hunting. In fact, he had a permanent reservation which must be cancelled at an inn that relied on men such as himself to fill their rooms to capacity each season. In future he'd have a very nice little property to which he'd come and to which he'd bring parties. Yes, he thought, looking around, it would be very pleasant indeed. . . . Eventually.

Everhart wandered along the once graveled paths between scraggly bushes and weedy flower beds. It occurred to him that his gardener at Heartland had two sons. The older would eventually take over at Heartland but the younger might be looking for his own gardens in which to play. He'd be the perfect choice to bring here. Another note was added to The List.

His lordship's wanderings took him toward a copse off to the side of the once-formal gardens. He was considering exploring the path through the trees when a modest explosion, the crackle and tinkle of broken glass, and an angry voice, yelling, "Blast and bedamned!" stirred him to immediate action. In a trice he found himself in a clearing before a long low slate-roofed, building. The windows to the right of the door were shattered, the pieces scattered across the clearing.

Muttering could be heard from inside so Everhart concluded that his uninvited guest, whom he assumed was the building's occupant, must be in one piece. He was debating whether he should stick his nose into the man's business when the door was flung open and a rather disheveled young gentleman, his face blackened and his hair singed, felt his way out.

The stranger blinked for a moment, then covered his eyes. "Damn!" He felt for the wall, backed against it, and slid down, laying his head on his bent knees. "Blast and double damned! Now what do I do?"

"Are you in need of help?"

The head rose, the face questing much as Everhart had seen a hunting dog sniff the air, the animal's vision of far less use to him than his nose.

"Your eyes?" he asked gently.

"I can't see," said the young man, exhibiting amazing sangfroid in a situation which should have sent him into a state of panic.

"I will help you to the house and call a doctor at once."

"I would appreciate the help to the house but—" There was a rueful note in the educated voice. "—if you knew him, you wouldn't threaten me with Dr. Robbins. Unless you are my enemy?"

"I am not. The doctor's a quack?"

"The doctor has two methods of treatment. Cupping and leaching. I can't believe either will do my eyes the least bit of good."

"I agree. May I suggest that, if you are restraining fears that you are permanently blind, it is early days?"

The head came up, the watering eyes staring blankly in the general direction of Everhart's voice. "What do you mean?"

"I have an army friend who happened to be within sight of a magazine which blew up. He was blinded by the flash but, gradually, began to see again. Eventually his vision was very nearly as good as new."

"Very nearly . . ."

"I'm sorry I cannot tell you it was exactly as new."

"But he could see?"

"Well enough for most things. It is true he could no

longer nick the pips in a playing card at twenty paces, a skill of which he'd been inordinately proud."

"You think I should not give up hope all at once?"

"I think we should give it time. His doctor recommended he rest in a dim room so that further light could do no more damage. I will guide you back to the Manor if you will allow me to do so and Hamish will see to your comfort."

"Hamish?"

"He's officially my valet but is, in actuality, far more. He'll turn his hand to anything and do a bang-up job of it. Once that involved rescuing me from pirates by whom I was captured. We were traveling in the Mediterranean and . . ." Everhart made a good story of it, taking Sedgewycke's mind off his troubles. "I could not do without Hamish, but the most important thing he may do at the moment is to see to your comfort."

"I didn't mean to be a nuisance when I decided to come here just as usual. Perhaps I should explain . . ."

"Not just now. I've been told you are an inventor and a budding engineer. I suspect that building is a laboratory which you've set up here and I understand that you could not very well whisk it away with ease. If you'll stand I'll give you my arm. Yes, just so. Now we'll be on the path through the spinney and then through the gardens. I'll try to choose a way which is not so overgrown we may not walk side by side. You are doing very well. You'll do, I think."

"My name is Sedgewycke. Aaron Sedgewycke."

"And I am Lord Everhart. Philip Hartford, at your service."

"Please call me Aaron. Under these circumstances it is ridiculous to stand on ceremony. Besides, I dislike the formal manners of our time and class. I much prefer the bonhomie one finds among the men with whom I work—worked—whenever they'd have me."

"With any luck you'll work with them again," soothed Philip. "I understand you had a part in building a Gothic stairway at Taymouth Castle." It was the right question to have asked and long before they reached the house Everhart knew far more than he'd ever wanted to know about the problems of construction which it had been necessary to overcome.

News of Sedgewycke's blindness soon reached Beverly Place. Georgi, hearing it from the housekeeper, went immediately in search of her cousin. It would not do, she thought, for Cassie to hear of it in public. The peahen would very likely give herself away.

The peahen wasn't to be found in the house. Georgi went out to the gardens and to the bower in which they'd talked that morning. As she approached, she heard voices. She recognized Elliot's high sneering tones and pressed her lips together. She hoped he'd not picked up the news in the village. If he were aware of his sister's infatuation—and Elliot had a way of discovering those things one most wished he'd never find out—he was very likely enjoying over-setting his sister's sensibilities. She moved nearer.

". . . Bloody all over, I heard," gloated Elliot.

Just as she'd feared, Cassie was near to fainting away. "Nonsense, Cassie," she said bracingly. "Sedgie won't even have bruises."

"I heard it in the village," said Elliot. "The groom from the Manor came into the tavern with the tale. All over blood. He swore it."

"Did he indeed? Then why does Mrs. Booth, whose niece has taken work at the Manor, say Sedgie walked into the house himself and that Lord Everhart tells them his problems are very likely only temporary."

Cassie, who was reviving under Georgi's bracing words, timidly asked, *"What* temporary problems?"

"There was a blast in his laboratory. Although he wasn't hurt in any other way, his eyes were bothered. He is to rest for some days in a darkened room."

"But he wasn't cut about? His face . . . ?"

Georgi sighed. "He wasn't cut at all. Neither his face nor anywhere else."

"The groom said . . ."

Georgi rounded on Elliot. "You've had your fun and frightened your sister out of what few wits she possesses. My grandfather will not approve of such ungentlemanly behavior. I wonder what he'll have to say to you—not that I can't imagine every word of it."

Elliot blenched. It hadn't occurred to him anyone would catch him out in his little game. He knew very well how unsportingly he had behaved, but he always found it impossible to resist putting pins in whenever an opportunity presented itself. His sister just happened to be one from whom he could always get a rise. But his grandfather had an even nastier tongue than his own. The old gentleman would flay strips from him. "You wouldn't . . ."

"I wouldn't tell him, you think? And why not? It is what you would do yourself, is it not?"

Elliot's skin took on an ashy hue. "I warn you, if you tell him anything at all you'll regret it!"

"Threats? I'll tell him that too. Oh, go away. You are decidedly *de trop.*" Georgi turned her back on her cousin, going over to sit beside Cassie and taking her cousin's cold hand into her own. "Sedgie will be quite all right."

"I must go to him," said the young woman with determination.

"Yes," agreed Georgi, "but not this evening. He needs

rest now, but I fear, unless he has changed a great deal, he will find convalescence exceedingly boring. Perhaps we might take him a bouquet or fruit from the succession houses. *Tomorrow,"* she added when Cassie jumped immediately to her feet ready to set off instantly. "For now you must collect yourself and prepare for dinner or we'll be late and, if you do not wish your mother to guess you are overset, you *must* put aside your concern."

"You say he'll be all right?"

Georgi crossed the fingers hidden in a fold of her skirt. "The word I have is that, given time, he'll recover. Cassie, your mother is a rather perspicacious woman. Has she no suspicion you are in love with Sedgie?" she asked, curious.

"Oh no. Not now. She thinks it all over with a long time ago and that I have forgotten him."

"Very good. But we must not rouse her suspicions. She will like us to visit the Manor because it will bring you into contact with Everhart, but will not like it if you are to see Sedgie for fear you will succumb again."

"But how may I succumb *again* when I was never over him?"

Georgi's eyes rolled up. When she was certain that her patience with her cousin had not quite withered away, she said, "Your mother doesn't know you are not over him, correct?" Cassie nodded and sudden understanding lit her eyes. Before the girl could ask another question Georgi went on. "I think we must throw dust in her eyes, Cassie. I will intimate at dinner that *I* am worried about Sedgie. I will talk of the times when I helped him in his experiments and how much I miss him when he is not living at the Manor. I believe your mother will put two and two together and get the required three."

Cassie raised her fingers and did some counting. "But, cousin, two and two are four."

"Yes, but if she is *misled,* the *three* she will come up with is that there is something between Sedgie and myself. Then she will not worry about *your* feelings for him, thinking *I* will keep him occupied and away from you."

"But there is *not?* You have no *tendre* for him?" Cassie's brows twisted into an intense frown.

"Not a jot or tittle of anything more than friendship."

"Oh. Although, when he is so wonderful, I do not see why you do *not.*" The frown disappeared, but there was still a look in Cassie's eyes that Georgi found unsettling. "You helped him in his experiments?" she asked.

"Yes." Georgi now had an inkling of what was in her cousin's head.

"What are experiments?" asked the dainty blonde, suspicion in her eyes, her shoulders stiff and head thrust forward belligerently.

Georgi, taken by surprise, laughed. "Experiments? You don't know what is meant by experimenting? You are joking, are you not?"

"No." The stubborn light in Cassie's eyes made Georgi sober quickly. "I want to know what you've been doing with my Sedgewycke."

"Cassie, I am not in love with Sedgie nor he with me and that is all you need to know. We *must* return to the house and prepare for dinner or face Grandfather's censure. He does not like tardiness, you know."

"Oh dear." Cassie had no wish to face her grandfather's anger, but she was still concerned about the relationship between her cousin and her love and torn between wishing to hurry and wishing to be reassured. "He doesn't love you? You are quite certain of that? He is so brilliant that I fear he will never think of me in the way I would wish because I have feathers where my brains should be." Again the glare of suspicion. *"You* don't have feathers. Mama says you are far too intelligent for your own good and, because of it, will never receive an offer from anyone you would accept and, in all likelihood, will find yourself on the shelf."

"I doubt I'll find that the disaster you think it should be."

"But you don't understand," objected Cassie. "I am very nearly the same age as you and if you are nearly on the shelf, then so am *I.*"

"Will wonders never cease: You *can* add two and two if it is important to you."

Confusion reigned again in Cassie's expression. "Whatever do you mean?"

"Never mind. It was unkind of me to tease you. Now, shall we return, quickly, to the house. Grandfather, you know . . ."

Having put that fear back into Cassie's head, and knowing how her cousin liked to primp, Georgi had hopes her cousin would forget about Sedgie long enough to make it through dinner without giving herself away. But, just in case, she promised herself she'd stay alert and draw attention to herself if it looked as if Cassie needed help.

Her worry was not unfounded: Elliot, who could never resist stirring waters to see what mud he might find, mentioned Sedgewycke had been injured. He kept his eyes on his sister and was as surprised as everyone else to hear Georgi shriek. "Sedgie? He's been hurt?" Elliot glared her way, his eyes narrowing and his mouth opening to reveal she was shamming it. She narrowed her gaze as well and then, quickly, flicked her eyes toward their grandfather. Elliot's mouth snapped shut. "Tell me! Tell me at once he isn't badly hurt!"

"It is believed he will recover," mumbled Elliot.

"Recover," insisted Georgi, shrewishly, "from what?"

"I was only told he was injured," said Elliot.

Georgi rose to her feet. "I must go to him at once . . ."

"Georgianna Thomasina, sit yourself down. Now. What is this nonsense? What are you about?" Her Aunt Anne frowned severely at her niece's odd behavior. "This is not like you, my dear."

Georgi noted the narrowing of her Aunt Melicent's eyes and wished she could force a blush. "I've never said anything . . ."

Lord Tivington decided it was time to take a hand. "I am tired of this subject. Tomorrow you may take the tilbury and visit him and see for yourself that he has taken no harm. You will take your cousin as chaperon." Melicent opened her mouth to object. "I do not wish you to visit Lord Everhart's house by yourself," added the devious gentleman at the head of the table, who was the only one to guess at Georgi's ploy. He had noted how Cassie blenched and had caught that significant moment when Georgi warned Elliot to behave. His lordship had learned to add at an early age.

Melicent, placated by the mention of Lord Everhart, promised herself a long chat with her daughter on just how she was to behave when she was chaperoning Georgi. There were nuances to the situation her nitwit of a daughter would surely miss, the most important of which was that here was an opportunity to thrust herself onto Lord Everhart under circumstances where, as host, he couldn't walk away.

Luckily for Cassandra, Aunts Anne and Marie maneuvered Melicent and their father to the whist table immediately after dinner, a proceeding made possible by the fact Lord Tivington had ordered that Booth *not* offer the port at table for so long as young George Elliot remained at the Place. There would be exceptions to the new rule, of course. When there were guests, for instance, port and snuff would appear as was customary once the women left the table. But, unless company joined them, Lord Tivington had no intention of sitting in the dining room alone with the bore his grandson had become and pretend polite interest in the things which interested the boy.

The grandson in question was not particularly shocked—was, in fact, relieved—to discover the change in custom. He preferred brandy to port and was, as well, desirous of having as little to do with his grandfather as that gentleman wished to do with him. This evening he was particularly pleased. He'd heard there was to be a cockfight and wished to depart for the village as early as possible so he'd miss none of it.

Everyone except Melicent finished the evening feeling fairly well satisfied. She had not had that talk with her daughter. But even she slept soundly, expecting to lecture the girl in the firmest possible fashion long before Georgi was ready to drive over to the Manor.

Melicent made her plans with the handicap of ignorance of Georgi's habits, which included rising at dawn most days. It wasn't easy rousing Cassie, however, or making her hurry her morning toilet, which, given she was to see her dearest Sedgewycke, would have been more prolonged than ever if Georgi hadn't chosen a dress practically at random and thrust it at her and then taken the brush from her cousin's dilatory hand and, with a few rapid twists and turns, produced a surprisingly satisfactory coiffure.

Cassie, impressed, wished to know how she'd done it. "Later, you idiot. Do you *wish* your mother to awaken before we are gone? Do you not realize she will have very specific instructions for your behavior while at the

Jeanne Savery

Manor and they will include an order you are to stay as far from Sedgie as possible?"

Cassie flew to the armoire, where she chose the first hat to come to hand. Only the fact that she did not own an unbecoming bonnet made her choice unexceptionable. For the first time in her flighty life she had no thought for her looks, but rushed from the room and down the back stairs, where she stopped in confusion. "Georgi, the carriage will be brought to the house, will it not? And did you not say we were to take flowers and fruit and, Georgi"—Cassie's eyes glistened—"I cannot help it, but I'm *hungry!*"

"The flowers are picked and in water. I searched out only the very best fruit. The horse is very likely waiting in harness just outside the kitchen and, as we pass through, I'll have Cook give you bread and cheese, which you may eat as we go." Georgi tipped her head. "Cassie, how is it that you are hungry? I hadn't thought about it, but I'd have guessed you'd have *no* appetite, worrying, as you appear to be, about Sedgie."

"When I'm worried I am ever hungry," confided the girl, a blush giving her cheeks a glow which had been missing. "I crept down in the night and ate a chicken wing and two tarts and a slab of bread with butter and blackberry jam and drank two glasses of milk and . . ."

"And that's enough. You make me feel quite ill. Maybe Cook should give you two pieces of bread and cheese," Georgi muttered as she led the way into the kitchens where all was abustle.

Preparations were under way for carrying morning trays and cans of hot water to the upper floor. No one was surprised to see Georgi but the sight of Cassie, up and dressed to go out at such an hour, so astonished the youngest maid she dropped her tray and was soundly scolded for a ninny.

The drive to the Manor was pleasant although Cassie obviously fretted. She actually stole an apple from the gift basket and gnawed it. "Georgi, does Grandfather approve of your friendship with Mr. Sedgewycke?" she asked. Her suspicions had been aroused again by Georgi's playacting at the dinner table the evening before, but she'd been so pleased that Lord Tivington said they were to go to the Manor she'd forgotten it till now.

"Cassie, get it into your head that Sedgie and I have never been anything but friends. I enjoyed learning from him because he was interested in things which did not interest Grandfather and, because of what I learned, I've been able to read the scientific papers Grandfather has sent from London. The latest was one on Animal Magnetism. Fascinating."

"I know nothing of Animal Magnetism," said Cassie in a small voice.

It occurred to Georgi that perhaps she was doing her cousin no favor by throwing her at Sedgie. Perhaps the attentions Sedgie had shown the girl were no more than a kindness on his part, although Georgi did not recall her old friend as being particularly *kind*. What if he took Cassie in disgust? Worse, what if he showed it? Cassie would be devastated. Worst of all, she might fall willingly into any plans her mother made for her and Lord Everhart, despair goading her to a disastrous marriage since she could not have the man with whom she'd fallen in love. Not that Georgi understood *that* either.

That is, she didn't until she set eyes on her old play fellow! "*Not* the great gawky fellow you described to me," said Lord Everhart in her ear as they stood apart from the chaise longue where Cassie was shyly greeting her blind swain. Georgi could not determine whether Sedgie was pleased to have her there or disturbed and unhappy by the visit. "Do not frown so. I will think you are jealous of your cousin if you do."

"I was wondering if perhaps sh—we had imposed her—ourselves where sh—*we* were not wanted."

Everhart had no difficulty untangling Georgi's unusually garbled speech. "If I read him correctly," said Everhart softly, "he is only upset that she finds him incapacitated in this way. He is not sorry to see her—not that that is the word one should use in the circumstances—and will be happy for her visit once he gets his pride in hand." Lord Everhart raised his voice. "Miss Beverly, when you finish talking over old times, you will find a book of William Shakespeare's plays lying on the table. I read from *All's Well That Ends Well* last evening and perhaps you might carry on with it."

"Hmm?" Cassie raised starry eyes. "Oh. Yes. Of course. Would you like that, Mr. Sedgewycke?" she asked.

"Not at the moment. Tell me more of your successes, Miss Beverly . . ."

"Yes, very reprehensible of us," said Lord Everhart as he removed himself and Georgi from the room, closing the door softly as he did so. "But I see no place for us in that terribly tiresome twosome. Are you trying to make a match there?"

"It is very likely impossible. Her parents—her mother, at least?"

"High in the instep? With me in the offing a mere Mister doesn't stand a chance, is that it? I am to understand, however, that I have been eclipsed in her eyes by that stripling?"

"But he is not a stripling, is he? In fact he has turned out very well, has he not? I admit it never occurred to me Sedgie would grow up to be an Adonis and I quite see why my cousin has lost her silly heart to him."

"And you? Will you lose your heart as well?" Everhart could not understand why he held his breath. She was little more than a child, after all . . . and her infant infatuations could be of no importance. . . .

"My *heart?* I doubt it. Sedgie and I know each other too well for that. He is more like a brother, I think. Not that I *know,* for I have none, and he is certainly nothing like poor Cassie's brother! Like a brother *should* be perhaps? Do I talk nonsense?"

"Nary a bit, child. In fact, that is a very mature thought for one so young as yourself." Having heard what he'd hoped to hear, Everhart now wondered why he treated his young friend so condescendingly. He shook his head, putting such questions aside. There was simply no sense in them. "Will you come into the gardens with me? Perhaps you like gardening and can tell me what ought to be done with them?"

"You should consult my Aunt Anne, my lord. She took the Place gardens in hand years ago. I believe she has something of a reputation among those who take such things seriously. The succession houses are also under her guidance and we have the most delicious things to eat all the year round because of her constant attention to their organization."

"But what do *you* think of gardens and gardening?"

Georgi glanced up and found her host's gaze upon her and wondered at its intensity. It did the strangest things to her pulse. Georgi looked away and told herself not to be a widgeon. "I'm old-fashioned in such things, my lord. When next you ride into the village take notice of the riot of blooms around the first cottage. *That* is my notion of an ideal garden, flowers of all shades and colors and scents all jumbled together. I cannot help you decide what to do with this, my lord." She gestured toward the long-ignored beds.

Everhart realized he'd been staring at her and turned away. "I'll very likely turn it over to a gardener and give him a free hand with it, but if you like, I'll tell him I wish a corner made into just such a garden as that which you described and you may visit it whenever you will. This is not an estate where I'll spend a great deal of time, you see, although I am becoming more and more aware of the advantages of owning it."

Georgi threw him a quick look but he was gazing off over the bluish hills of the Cotswolds. She decided it had not been a flirtatious comment and wondered why she felt depressed by that knowledge.

"I hunt, you know," he said diffidently, suspecting she held strong but contrary views on the subject. "It will be good to have a home to come to rather than mere rack and manger at the inn which has, until now, had my patronage. One is overcharged and underfed and terribly crowded. Sometimes several people—total strangers—sleep in the same bed! This will be much nicer. Especially once I've put up some decent stabling."

"Now *there* I *do* have notions. I've never seen Sir Minnow's facilities."

"Facilities? My dear child, Sir Minnow had no use for *facilities*. He did not house his cattle in sheds, but I swear the current stabling is very little better. Would you like to see for yourself?"

A short time later Georgi stopped before the sagging doors of the small stable and, hands on hips, looked around. "Good heavens."

"Exactly."

"Oh dear."

"I couldn't have said it better."

Georgi glanced at him, her eyes twinkling. "I am very certain you *could,* my lord. I could myself if I weren't attempting to play the part of a lady." When he opened his mouth, obviously ready to encourage her to lay aside that role, Georgi shook her head, laughing. "No, you will not goad me into saying that the old scab-bag let all go to the devil and that you must immediately tear that down and begin from scratch." Her brows pulled together. She shifted her weight to one foot and laid a finger on her mouth.

Lord Tivington could have told Lord Everhart that Georgi was plotting. Lord Everhart, a knowing 'un, didn't need the telling: He guessed. "Tell me the worst at once," he demanded. "It will take all my modest fortune to put up the operation which you are now designing for me, will it not?"

His question broke Georgi's concentration. "Oh, I daresay not all of it." She turned back to the setting. "I am partial to the U-shaped form of stabling although many object on several grounds." Again she looked at him. "What is your opinion, my lord?"

"It is a good construction in that the head groom can see all that goes on about him. But it has the problem that in the winter the grooms must do much of their work in the cold, which is not the case when the stabling is in an enclosed barn. Nor, in winter, are the animals so warm as when, in a barn, each animal contributes body heat for them all."

"But if one gates off the open end to prevent drafts then it is not so very bad, is it?"

"Expensive, however, since I'll be here only during the hunting season."

"Not even for the cubbing?"

"Unlikely." He looked down at her. Perhaps she didn't object to the hunt? "Do you hunt or does your grandfather think you too young?"

"I could if I would, but I don't care for it." She turned away. It was thought a particular oddity in her that she objected to the traditional way of dealing with an excess population of foxes. "I see I must confess or you will not understand. I do not approve of running down a poor creature and allowing dogs to tear it to pieces. It is not at all proper to feel sorry for a fox and I agree they must not be allowed to become pests, but wouldn't hunting them with a gun as one does pheasants do as well?"

"Most enjoy the riding. You could leave before the end, could you not?"

"But if I were to join in at all, wouldn't that suggest I approve? I *don't,* you see."

"I see you think it a moral problem. Perhaps as you become older and grow less sensitive you will not feel so strongly about it. Shall we agree we'll not argue about it? It seems a terrible waste of a lovely day."

She smiled ruefully. "But won't we argue just as much about the style of stable you should build?"

He laughed. "Perhaps, but it seems less stressful and more enjoyable. Do you think there should be rooms for the grooms attached to the barns?"

"Above the barn which crosses the bottom of the U," she said promptly. "The rooms should have windows and not be too small. I've always thought it ridiculous the way a wealthy family has living space to waste and then puts their servants into rooms no bigger than a minute. Grandfather knocked the walls out between every other room in the attics where the women servants live. They each have a bed and dresser as always, but also a wash stand for those who wish it and a chair. Worn sheets and old clothes were provided to any who wish to braid themselves a rug. And they each have a mirror so they may ensure neatness before leaving their rooms." Georgi grimaced. "The men servants have always had larger rooms. Why do men always get the best of everything in this world?"

"Do we?" He raised a hand to stop her when, noting how her eyes glittered, he realized he had spoken unthinkingly. "I suppose we do. It is because we've always ruled things, do you not think?"

"But we've had excellent queens. There were Elizabeth and Mary, for instance. *They* each ruled with an iron fist. I do not see why women who are not royal must be retiring and without a thought in their heads."

"My dear, it is obvious. If you had a thought in your head, you might see that you *could* rule. You must see we gentlemen cannot allow you to do that!" He snorted, a rueful sound. "We don't *wish* to allow it," he continued, "but on occasion a woman rules. Think of your aunt Melicent. She runs her husband with that iron fist of which you spoke. I prefer to say she has a heavy hand on the reins, myself."

"I am inconsistent," admitted Georgi ruefully. "I do not like my aunt's managing ways. Nevertheless, I do not see why I, for instance, could not do better in Parliament than the man who holds our local seat. He is ignorant and uncaring. He stands for election because his wife wishes to cut a dash in London during the weeks Parliament sits." She shook her head. "It is not quite a rotten borough, my lord, but he provides the necessary treating, a tun of ale, and an ox for roasting, to buy the votes he needs."

"Something of the sort is, far too often, the case. In a constituency it is usually not what one knows, but whom. Even though you may know the *what,* Georgi, you may not know the *whom.*"

"In my case it is not what *or* whom, but only that I am female that I may not do as I wish."

"Just what *do* you wish, since I'd guess it is not to run for Parliament?"

"Oh, I don't know." She *couldn't* tell him the *truth.*

"Maybe I'd be a doctor?" She touched her tongue to her lip, thinking quickly. "Have you read of Jenner's work? And do you know why some midwives lose fewer mothers than others to childbed fever?"

"I have certainly read Jenner's theories concerning inoculations. I have not heard why new mothers die of the fever, however."

"Neither do I know for certain, but I've observed that Goodwife Hammer is a very clean woman while Goodie Moore is exceedingly dirty in her habits. It is Goodwife Hammer who loses the fewer patients."

"Dirt makes them sick? But we are around dirt all our lives, child, so how can that be?" It occurred to Lord Everhart that this was an exceedingly odd conversation to hold with a young girl—with anyone for that matter! But it was surprisingly interesting so he wasn't about to point out the oddity of it. "Do you know?"

"I don't know *how* but I believe it does somehow cause childbed fever. Have you never had a sore or scrape which you could not clean immediately and it becomes inflamed and sometimes puss-filled?"

"I have seen such," said his lordship, his eyes narrowing. Could the chit be on to something? He would discuss it with someone who had greater experience and was, therefore, able to judge more nearly than a young girl who was barely beyond her childhood. His conscience smote him. Childbed fever indeed! How could he be talking of such things with a young and innocent girl? As interesting as he found their discussion, he'd best change it. "We have gotten onto a subject which I feel certain your aunts would think improper. Instead, why do you not tell me more of what you think I should do about my new stabling? That is far more important to me just now than which midwife to choose to have charge of the birthing of my wife's first child."

"Your wife?" Georgi turned startled eyes toward the man, who was idly surveying what would be the site of his new stables. "You are married?" Now why, she wondered, did that thought make her chest tighten, *so*.

"Wife?" Everhart looked down at the girl staring at him in such a worried way. "What wife?"

"The one you mentioned."

"How could I have mentioned a wife when I have none?"

"Of course you have not or Cassie could not wed you." Georgi blinked. "That's all right then."

"What is all right?"

A bewildered expression flitted over the girl's features. "You know, my lord, I haven't the least notion? Now about those stables . . ."

Five

Several days passed with the two girls spending each morning at Minnow Manor. They enjoyed themselves very much, but Georgi noticed a speculative look on Aunt Melicent's face the evening before, and occasionally she felt guilty leaving Sedgie so much alone with Cassie. Therefore she suggested that Lord Everhart take her cousin for a stroll in the gardens while she read to her old friend. Cassie glared at her, but when Lord Everhart offered his arm she went off docilely enough. The look of boredom which immediately took up residence on Everhart's face, however, didn't suggest they'd be gone long.

Georgi jumped in. "Sedgie, would you rather I kept Cassie home?"

"Home? What can you mean?"

"I mean the necessity of remaining polite to such an empty-headed little fizgig must strain your sensibilities when you already find yourself worried about yourself."

"Frank as ever," said Aaron with a grin. "Do not worry *your* head, Georgi. I am perfectly happy and find her prattle distracting and—you may laugh if you wish—entertaining!"

Georgi choked back the expected chuckle. "You are not bamming me?" she asked suspiciously.

Aaron sobered. He reached a hand toward her and

Georgi took it between her own. "You will laugh still more when I tell you I fell in love with her the first time I saw her. She was a fairy princess, Georgi." A dreamy look filled the blind eyes. "Her mother had dressed her in pale pink with silver threads running through it. She had a silvery headdress and carried a silver thread reticule. Her little slippers were silver too. If she had had wings she could have flitted around the chandeliers laughing at all of us big awkward humans."

"I see you have it bad, Sedgie."

"Very bad. And hopelessly. Allow me these few days to make memories, Georgi." He squeezed her hand. "All too soon her mother will discover what is toward and will interfere, taking her from my orbit. Again." He chuckled wryly. "Do you know it has become almost impossible to have so much as a country dance with my love at the *tonish* balls we both attend? Her mother keeps a close eye on her."

"But, Sedgie, how can you have deep feelings for someone who cannot enter into your interests?"

"I do not need to think deep thoughts all day every day. I like her chatter about clothes and the squeezes she's attended and light gossip about the people we both know. It relaxes me."

Georgi frowned. "Love is a funny thing, is it not?" As she spoke, the door opened. Georgi looked around to see her aunt's gaze fixed on their clasped hands. Without embarrassment Georgi let go. "Aunt Melicent. Have you come to visit Mr. Sedgewycke? You do know each other, do you not?"

Sedgie composed his startled face and stood up. "Lady Melicent."

"Mr. Sedgewycke. I see you are well entertained already," purred that lady with satisfaction. "I will not put myself forward into your tête-à-tête, but will find Lord

Everhart." She reached for the doorknob, but it moved
away from her, opening to allow her daughter and his
lordship entry.

"Hamish told us you had arrived, Lady Melicent.
How are you?" Lord Everhart didn't wait for a response,
moving into the room and turning his back to the company. "Very good, Hamish," he said and beamed. "Set
that chair there, if you will. Two more are required. And
then, a tea tray I believe." He reached for the quizzing
glass with which Hamish had managed to supply him
that morning. It had been an irritation to him until this
moment. Now he found it handy to twiddle and turn,
or to swing gently to and fro. Soon the furniture was
arranged to suit him. He seated Cassie beside
Sedgewycke on one side and Georgi on the invalid's
other side. He seated himself between Georgi and Lady
Melicent. "There. Aren't we cozy? How are you enjoying your stay in the country Lady Melicent . . . ?"

Somehow Lord Everhart controlled the ensuing conversation. Georgi was amused by his expertise and
studied his methods. They were, perhaps, a trifle ruthless, but they answered well enough. Lady Melicent was
unable to so much as hint at a personal topic, concerning either her daughter and Lord Everhart or her niece
and Mr. Sedgewycke. But it was done so smoothly, the
lady wasn't even particularly insulted when she found
herself being escorted, along with her daughter, to her
carriage.

Lord Everhart returned to Sedgewycke's sitting room
to discover Georgi holding her sides and laughing im-
moderately. Sedgie was chuckling as well. "I hope
someone will allow me in on the jest. I, too, would
enjoy a laugh," said Lord Everhart sternly, "especially
since I've worn myself to a thread, putting forth so

much effort for our mutual benefit. I've *earned* a laugh."

"It was the look on Aunt's face, my lord. That bemused look. I've never seen her so betwattled."

Everhart's brows arched. "Betwattled? What a word."

"Like an old rooster I once saw which had been doused with a bucket of water. He didn't quite know what had happened, which is certainly true of my aunt. Unfortunately Cassie got a trifle carried away last night—talking about *you,* Sedgie." Georgi threw him an apologetic look which he, in his blindness, could not see. "I feared Aunt had become suspicious."

"So you sent Cassie off with me this morning," said Everhart. "You expected her mother's visit. I thought you were on my side, Georgi."

"I am! I did think Aunt Melicent might visit. It seemed to me better if she found Cassie with you, my lord, and me with Sedgie."

"You are a born conniver and always will be, Georgi Thomasina," scolded Sedgewycke, but the laughter in his voice softened the reprimand.

"Well, yes, I suspect that is so," said Georgi apologetically. "But, it seems to me a much better thing to arrange things so that we not get into a row, than to do nothing and allow it to happen."

"I," said Lord Everhart, "feared I had angered you somehow that you punished me with your cousin's company. We have nothing to say to each other. What's worse, she says nothing at such great length," he finished ruefully.

"You should have asked her to talk about Sedgie," scolded Georgi. "She'd have had plenty to say on that subject, too, but you needn't have listened to her as she rattled on because, when she talks about Sedgie, she doesn't require an answer."

"So I discovered. It answered very well. But I was never more pleased than when Hamish came to tell me of her mother's arrival. I immediately returned us to the house."

"You erred, however, when you sent her off home with her mother. My aunt will, from the moment the carriage began to roll, catechize poor Cassie on how she is getting on with yourself. It would have been better to keep them apart."

"But I could feel she was ready to suggest something the peahen and I might do together and that seemed a more immediate and greater danger."

"I do not care to hear Miss Beverly spoken of in the derogatory terms you use, my lord," said Aaron, who had closely followed the fast-paced exchange, his head turning from one to the other—or very nearly at them.

It was disconcerting to find oneself not-quite-looked-at and Georgi hoped, for Sedgie's sake, it would soon be a thing of the past. Sedgie had admitted he could now see a flicker of light in his right eye when looking straight at a candle in an otherwise dark room. Surely that was a hopeful sign his vision would return.

"Sedgie," said Georgi, "don't you start. There is enough on my plate without the need to play peacemaker between you two. Besides, it is not at all polite to rip up at your host."

Aaron flushed. "You are correct, Georgi. It is not."

"Oh I don't mind," said Everhart. "I keep forgetting you *like* the peahen." This was said with a such wry twist to his tone that Georgi laughed outright and Aaron could not suppress a chuckle. "But I should not call her so. If one is to talk of manners, it is not proper for a host to say naughty things about an invited guest. Now if the guest is *not* invited, of course, one may say what one chooses . . ." Again Aaron choked back laughter.

". . . and I choose to wonder at your good sense in choosing a peahen to love!"

"I have no choice," said Aaron with great simplicity. "I did no more than set eyes on her than I was lost to all reason. She is beautiful. She is graceful, and so . . ."

"Wanting in her attic?"

"But that makes no difference, does it? A woman is not required to have intelligence."

Georgi and Everhart exchanged a look, reminding, each the other, of the conversation they'd had on that topic. "*I* am a woman, Sedgie, and *my* head is not empty of all but *tonish* gossip. *I* am not lacking in my upper works."

Aaron frowned. "Your grandfather has done you no service, educating you as he has. You will find it difficult if not impossible to find a husband to care for you, Georgi. How will you go on? Think of the difficulty when your grandfather is no longer there to indulge you. What will you do?"

"I doubt very much my grandfather will leave me destitute. I now see why he insists I learn the rudiments of what happens to one's investments on 'Change and how to talk to an agent. He is preparing me to deal with my inheritance in case it becomes necessary for me to do so."

"Deal-with-your-inheritance? *Yourself?*" Sedgewycke blanched. "Georgi, it isn't done. Surely he is not such a fool as to put you in control of your fortune. A trustee . . . better, *two* trustees. Georgi . . ." He stared blindly. "Georgi," he asked in a milder tone, "are you *growling?*"

Everhart loosed the laughter he was manfully attempting to restrain. "Sedgewycke, I thought you *knew* Miss Beverly. It is too bad you can not see her. She is red in the face and her hands are clenched until her knuckles are white and I greatly fear that she will give one or both of us the facer we deserve. Easy, child," he said soothingly, "I am teasing you. I do not believe you will be incapable of dealing with your finances when you've had a year or two more of training."

Fortunately, the appellation of *child* reminded Georgi that Everhart had no notion of her true age and she stopped herself ripping up at him as she'd wished to do but was unable to do toward Sedgie, handicapped, as he was, by his blindness. It also occurred to her she had been rather inattentive to her grandfather's lectures on the maintenance of one's fortune. She found them a dead bore and tended to think, instead, of her writing and the difficulty she'd next arrange for her beautiful, naive, and very likely, featherheaded, heroine. In future, she promised herself, she'd pay attention.

Sedgie had begun to look worn around the edges and Georgi suggested they go away and allow him a rest. The next hour was spent touring the house, with Georgi suggesting all sorts of wild changes Everhart might make to provide himself with a proper bachelor establishment. Everhart was in whoops—until she shocked him by pointing out there were no mirrors over the beds in the guest bedrooms.

"Where do you learn of such things?"

"You have met Elliot, of course, but do you know George Vincent?"

"Oh." Everhart scowled. "Do you mean to tell me he has spoken of such things to you?"

"I asked him to describe a bordello to me."

"Georgi, even if you asked, he had no business telling you about the decor in a bordello! How could he have been so insensitive to your innocence? How could he have had so little care for your sensibilities?"

Georgi used a word learned from the same source which neatly expressed her feelings.

"Georgi." His lordship grasped her shoulders and shook her. "If you weren't so young, I'd have to assume you the most depraved young woman I've ever met. You must not allow anyone to know you are aware of such things. They would take all sorts of encroaching fancies. They might mistake you for . . ." He stopped, unable to think of a word that wasn't forbidden to him when speaking to a gently bred female.

Georgi had no such inhibitions. "Haymarket ware? A soiled dove?"

"Your cousin has much to answer for!"

"I learned the latter from my grandfather," she said demurely.

"You *didn't.*"

"Yes. You see he doesn't believe in protecting women from the harsh side of life. When I overheard a conversation between my aunts which I didn't understand about an acquaintance who had brought herself to ruin by her own folly, I asked him to explain. I think I was thirteen at the time. He didn't go into detail, you understand, but he told me how horrible the world is for women who must make their own way. Too many women have no choice at all, do they, but to cater to the whims and desires of some man who will then walk away and forget them?"

"I've never thought of it in quite that way . . . not that I've ever had much to do with such women myself. Not the sort who haunt the streets, that is." He flushed when he realized what he'd admitted, and, finding he still held her, shook her again. "Blast it, Georgi, you have *me* doing it. This is *not* a proper conversation for us to have."

She chuckled. "I cannot hold you at arm's length, my lord. You are too stimulating a conversationalist and I admit I forget to mind my tongue when conversing with you. In the past, you see, there has been no one but Grandfather and Vincent to whom I may speak freely. I have fallen into the way of it with you so gradually I hadn't noticed. If you wish, I will try to curb my tendency to say whatever is in my head. It will not be easy, however."

"Better me than someone less trustworthy. But you must remember, brat, it is not acceptable behavior with anyone else." Once again he shook her, but lightly this time. "Will you promise me?"

"Only to Grandfather, Vincent, and you will I speak so freely," she promised, her eyes holding his.

"Not Vincent. I don't approve of Vincent."

"Do not say that to me, Everhart," said Georgi, suddenly serious. "I am aware of his reputation, but he has always been kindness itself to me. I will not allow anyone to call him bad names in my presence. I do not believe he is evil, as my Aunt Anne insists, and, although he *may* be depraved, as Aunt Marie whispers, I know he has a good heart and can be very patient and exceedingly generous. I haven't a notion why he persists in hiding that positive side of his character. It is almost as if he revels in seeing how much he may make people swallow and I've often scolded him for it."

Everhart tipped his head, recalling a time he'd seen Vincent Beverly casually draw the fire of one of society's less-liked peers from the head of a green boy who had, not knowing how, gotten on the man's bad side. Vincent had been so successful the peer had called *him* out. It had not been Vincent who disappeared from society for a time.

Had Beverly stepped in on purpose to save the lad? Carefully going through the whole scene from beginning to end, Everhart concluded he had. His eyes came back into focus and he realized Georgi was frowning, her gaze fixed on his face, the flesh around her eyes revealing a certain tension which gave her a much too mature look for a child. Everhart realized his hands were on her shoulders and felt an unprecedentedly intense wish to pull her into his embrace, hold her head against his chest until she relaxed, and then tip up her chin for a kiss. An exceedingly thorough kiss followed by . . .

Instantly Everhart released his grip on Georgi and stepped back. What was the matter with him that he wished to make love to a young and untried girl? Perhaps *Vincent* was not so depraved as Miss Marie Beverly believed, but was he himself developing such tendencies in his old age? He felt prickles under his skin, a sure sign the blood had left his face. Surely he was not one of those men who, the older they became, began choosing younger and younger women until they were bedding mere children!

'Everhart? Are you ill?"

"Ill?" Perhaps he was. Yes. He was ill. "Georgi, I do not feel just the thing. Perhaps you should go home now and come again another day."

"Another day? Not tomorrow?"

Not tomorrow? Perhaps not. He would *not* allow himself to disintegrate into a dirty old man, but if he would not, then he must reorder his mind, get himself firmly in hand. "Tomorrow I'll be busy with builders, Georgi. We'll be discussing the new stables." It was something he'd intended leaving in Hamish's hands, but was the only excuse he could think of, given his bemused state. "And the next day I must see Sir Minnow's solicitor about some business I do not understand." That, at least was true, although he'd intended waiting until after the girls' daily visit to ride into Oxford and find the man. "I'm sorry," he added, seeing the disappointment in her eyes. He, too, felt disappointed. He bit the corner of his lip, determined to say no more. It would not do to encourage the brat, or to give encouragement to those sensations he'd discovered in himself!

"I suppose I'd better be off, then. You will rest?" she asked, the worry still evident in her eyes.

"Rest?" Everhart remembered he'd admitted to feeling ill. "I'll rest. Do not worry your head about me, child. I will be just fine very soon." *Or, if not,* he thought, *I'll allow neither you nor anyone else to guess it! Ever.*

"Please do. I have so few friends who enter into my interests, who laugh at the things at which I laugh, and who enjoy the things I enjoy, I could not bear to lose a single one of you."

"Friends . . ."

"Are we not?"

Again he saw that worry. "Go home, Georgi. Of course we are friends!" He flipped his finger against her nose and forced himself to grin at her. She seemed satisfied, her expression lightening, and he heaved a secret sigh of relief.

"London? Brighton? But *why?*" Lady Melicent asked her father-in-law. "You never go to Brighton, and you always have your solicitor come to you. Nor do I understand why you must go just now when I hoped we might plan a party to entertain Lord Everhart."

Lord Tivington had just announced he was leaving in the morning and had been greeted by shocked silence until Melicent dared speak what was in everyone's mind. "Is it necessary that you understand?" he asked blandly, looking up from the duck he was neatly deboning.

A masterful set-down, thought Georgi. *Will it answer?* It did not.

"I do not like it when I do not understand a thing," said Melicent. "You *never* rake around the countryside. Why should you just now?"

"Why should I not?"

Lady Melicent blinked. "Your age . . ."

Lord Tivington glared at her. "I am in sound health. If I were racing off to set a new record for the time between Oxford and London, then I'd see where you might think I'd reached my dotage, but since I will travel in a well-sprung carriage, will not attempt too many miles in a day, and will have Hickman to see to my needs, I will not have you—" he glanced around the table "—or *anyone* telling me such a journey is impossible."

Aunt Marie surprised everyone. "Why do you not take Georgi Thomasina with you? I know you have business to which you must attend, but she may see something of the country. Most importantly you may take her to Mrs. Mary Ann Bell's shop in Bloomsbury where she may order a new gown which is more in style." Everyone stared at the old blue muslin evening gown which Georgi had thrown on more because it was easy to don and she was late than that it had, or perhaps had *ever* had, a jot of style. "The semiannual Assembly at the rooms in Oxford is all too soon now. I had thought to order her something new from Mrs. Becket as usual, but I think a London gown more suitable this year." Marie had observed Lord Everhart's interest in Georgi and had dreams of a brilliant future for her niece, although she'd have allowed herself to be nibbled to death by ducks before revealing a hint of her hopes.

Not having that hint, everyone blinked, and proceeded

to chew out what meaning they could from the bones of her words. Georgi frowned. Lady Melicent's eyes narrowed and she really looked at her niece, as if trying to imagine what the girl would look like if appropriately gowned and her hair arranged stylishly. She didn't like what rose in her imagination. Cassie beamed, nodding her head in encouragement to her cousin with no notion that she invited competition. Cassie was an incomparable, and so far as she knew, there *was* no competition. Elliot, not so perceptive as his mother, mumbled something about making silk purses out of sows' ears, and Aunt Anne simply nodded her head to show she agreed, amazing as that fact was, with her sister.

Lord Tivington looked at Georgi. He sat back in his chair and rubbed his chin, his eyes on her. "Why not?" he said at last, his cogitations complete. "We should be gone no more than ten days, I think. Mrs. Bell will have to manage without the many fittings to which she is accustomed. Georgi, you must be ready to leave at dawn. If you have finished with what is on your plate—"

Georgi looked down to see she had, in her agitation, made a hash of the food there.

"—you may be excused to pack."

"There is another course . . ." exclaimed Marie.

"I am no longer hungry, Aunt Marie. If we leave so early, I must ask that I be excused." Georgi did not wait for permission, but rushed from the room in a less than ladylike way. Leave the Place? Go to London? *Brighton?* But she didn't wish to go . . . although if what she'd seen in Everhart's face had truly been revulsion, then perhaps it was best she do so.

Why could she not learn to bite her tongue? Why had she allowed herself to be so carried away by her teasing that she revealed knowledge any properly brought-up young lady could not possibly know? Everhart would not, thought Georgi crossly, have batted an eye at another man suggesting such things to him. He would have laughed and taken it all in good part—and perhaps, as a joke, have had one room prepared in just that fashion for that particular friend's use! But if a gently bred female intimated she knew of the existence of the earthier side of life, then she was beyond the pale! Sedgie would have been so shocked he'd never again have spoken to her. She'd believed Everhart above such pettiness. She'd erred. He was not. And now he wished to sever the connection.

Georgi slumped in her window seat, her head clutched between her hands. She groaned: Having lost his lordship's friendship, Georgi realized it was far more than mere companionship that she wished from him. It was bad enough she had disobeyed Grandfather's order that she not succumb to Everhart's charm, but through her thoughtlessness she had ruined all hope of it ever coming right!

But . . . had he not, just for a moment, been about to kiss her? She was absolutely and positively certain he had, which was silly since she'd no experience by which to judge. And he hadn't done so, of course. Not only had he not kissed her, he'd pushed her away and proceeded to make up ridiculous excuses so that she not visit soon, time in which he might discover reasons for denying her altogether.

Georgi had never understood how girls like Cassie could moon over a beau. Now, the sudden and unwanted revelation of her emotions unsettling her normal self-control, she found it quite an easy thing to do. Mooning must be a natural talent with which women were born, she decided, because here she was, mooning over Everhart with no effort on her part at all. Perhaps, she scolded herself, she was meant to suffer this way, a sort of punishment because she scorned such behavior in others. Ignorance, it was said, was bliss. How true. She'd been blissfully unaware how terribly painful unrequited love could be. She stood up, looked around, hunting distraction.

London . . . yes. Now she wanted to go to London. And mooning wouldn't get her packing done. To go. To be gone. Far, far away. . . for ten days at least? Georgi rang for a footman and asked him to bring a small trunk and a portmanteau to her room. She also asked that May Hickman, the aunts' abigail, be sent to her. It wasn't that she had so much to pack that she *required* help to save time, as that, having never before done it, she hadn't a notion how to go about it!

Learning a new skill helped push her newly discovered tender feelings for Everhart to the back of her mind. Travel and new experiences would also help, she told herself. Surely by the time they returned she would have recovered from the worst of it, she decided almost cheerfully.

Even Cassie could have told Georgi that she was, although she knew it not, still protected by ignorance. And bliss . . .

Six

Georgi was shocked by the press of traffic, the noise, and the dirt everywhere in London. She and her grandfather threaded a way through vehicles of all shapes and sizes, vendors of anything and everything, and pedestrians, both those strolling aimlessly and others making a firm way toward a particular destination. Progress to their appointment with Mrs. Bell was slow. "How can so many people manage to live together in one place?"

"*This* is not particularly crowded. During the Season, the number of carriages and pedestrians doubles—perhaps triples." Georgi shook her head, muttering that it was not possible. "You will discover for yourself, my dear, when we return in the spring."

"Must we?" Georgi thought of meeting Lord Everhart on his own ground, so to speak, and shivered. Coward, she thought. Besides, she scolded herself, she'd have expunged these silly feelings for the man long before the spring Season rolled around. Morosely, she answered her own question. "I suppose we must."

"Yes," said her grandfather with a small sigh. "I fear we must. It was very bad of you," he said, the corners of his lips turning upward, "to reach such a great age even I must admit it necessary. Why could you not have remained a child, Georgi?"

"Take a leaf from Lord Everhart's book, Grandfather,

and convince yourself that is exactly what I am. He doesn't find it difficult." Even Georgi heard the bitterness in her tone. She flushed. "If you could, then I need not return to this pestilential place."

It was not the first time Everhart's name had come into their conversation. Georgi would have been shocked if she'd realized how often she mentioned him. Lord Tivington, awake on every suit, came to the unavoidable conclusion his beloved granddaughter had had her first encounter with the game of hearts. Everhart would not, he believed, come to the point with her. The man was too wary to be caught by a green girl. It was too bad of him, too, when he'd promised he'd not harm the child . . . child? He frowned. *Why*, he wondered, did Everhart think her a child?

Georgi was late maturing, his thoughts continued, but she was not a child. It would require an exceptional man to perceive how special she was, though, and Lord Tivington didn't think Everhart the man. Actually, he despaired of finding such a one before ever beginning the search. More and more, Lord Tivington feared his selfishness with regard to Georgi had ruined her for a conventional marriage. He had done his granddaughter a disservice and now must make what amends he could, ensuring that her future be as comfortable as was possible in a society in which the only proper role for a woman was wife and mother. One of his tasks in London was to have his solicitor rewrite the portion of his will pertaining to his beloved Georgi.

His lordship's cogitations were necessarily put aside when his coachman pulled up before a discreetly painted doorway. Nothing more than a small brass plaque announced it was Mrs. Bell's place of business. Georgi's introduction to the fashionable modiste was brief and to the point. "Madam," said his lordship bluntly, "my granddaughter is in need of a wardrobe. Not the extensive one she'll require next spring for her Season, but one suitable to modish country living and the limited society one finds between Oxford and Cheltenham. It is understood?" The woman famous for her direction of the fashion department for the magazine *La Belle Assemblée* ceased her turning and poking at Georgi and nodded. "Do not make of her a chit fit only for the muslin company which appears to be the extreme of current style. I wish a lady when you finish, but with that touch of *something* most women have if it can only be pointed up."

"It will not be difficult, my lord. She is perfection. Tiny but rounded in all the correct places—not that anyone would know it when she wears such a *thing* as this." Mrs. Bell tweaked Georgi's sleeve. "One is not required to pad her dresses here—" She waved toward Georgi's bust. "—nor pretend she has what she has not here." The hand patted Georgi's bottom. "Still better, one need not conceal that which should not exist at all. You laugh, child? You think it amusing, the problems lesser women suffer? Ah, you've no compassion for the wallflower who is dumpy or frumpy or knows not the colors which improve a sallow skin. It is an art, dressing the woman who needs help. Bah!" Mrs. Bell threw up her hands. "Dressing *you*, why the least of my apprentices could do it. Go away, my lord Tivington. We will discuss colors and materials and I'll teach your granddaughter what will flatter her and what to avoid. Go! Go! You are decidedly *de trop*, my lord."

Lord Tivington gave strict orders that his granddaughter was to be returned to Grillon's Hotel by hackney carriage, accompanied by one of the mantua maker's more mature sewing women. The woman was not to return to Mrs. Bell until she had seen his Georgi to her sitting room and that she was settled with a light meal and a book. "I will return well before dinner,

Georgi, but that's later than usual here in town. Do not expect me any time before seven of the clock."

"Now you will *go,* my lord." Mrs. Bell bristled, her arm extended and her finger pointing.

His lordship grinned. "I'm off. Georgi, close your mouth. You should have guessed I'd not bring you to town for no more than the one gown suggested by your aunt. Yes, yes, madam, I'm gone! I'm gone!" And he was.

At first Georgi found it all very interesting. She had never seen so many fabrics in one place. Nor such quality. But Mrs. Bell lectured, talking until Georgi's head ached. It ached worse when she realized she was considering how Lord Everhart might like her in one design or another.

The situation was no better when they removed to the fitting rooms. In fact, it was worse. She was forced to stand immobile, dressed only in her chemise, a garment the modiste disparaged as fit only for the ash bin. Swaths of material were flung around her, pins put in here and there, and eventually the material removed by a harassed gray-haired woman to still another room, from which Georgi heard the babble of soprano voices and stifled laughter. She wished she could think of a reason to laugh.

Finally the last length of material had been shaped, the last pin poked in, and, hopefully, the last lecture given. Georgi suspected she should have paid more attention, guessing few were privileged to receive such an education from the likes of Mrs. Bell. But the woman had been repetitive and Georgi believed she'd not missed too many nuggets while attempting to avoid the chaff.

Mrs. Bell took her next to a small private sitting room and ordered much needed refreshment. "Now," she said, seating herself at a small table and bidding Georgi to do likewise, "we will discuss what is required in the way of scarves and reticules and shoes and such."

Georgi accepted a cup of very hot tea from the gray-haired woman. "Madam," she said, turning to her mentor, "I didn't realize dressing was so complicated."

"Complicated? Dressing is an *art*. If one has aptitude, ah that is a precious talent indeed. You, I believe, have it. Even that despicable gown of no fit and the insufferable hat in which you arrived, you wore them with a certain style. You carry yourself well and you do not cringe or show false modesty. It is well. With proper gowns—which won't include this thing we have found for you to wear now. You must give it away, my child, just as soon as your new gowns arrive—but as I say, with proper gowns and a new style for your hair you may hope to join the ranks of the incomparables."

Georgi was startled by such a thought. "My *cousin* is the beauty in the family, not *me*," she stated firmly if ungrammatically.

"Miss Cassandra is a beauty in the classic English mode. You are more a Pocket Venus." Georgi made a moue of distaste. "It does not please you to be such a one?" asked Mrs. Bell, a faint edge of danger in her tone.

"I believe you too honorable to reveal that I am that terrible creature, a bluestocking so I'll admit I know about the goddess the Romans called Venus. And, although it is a matter of indifference to me if I am known as patron of flower gardens, I do not care to be considered a goddess of *love!*"

"Flowers? What has Venus to do with flowers?"

"It is said to be one of the goddess's aspects. I enjoy *looking* at flowers, you understand, but don't require that I make for you a garden!"

The modiste was bewildered by what seemed to her a nonsequitur. "Garden? Flowers? You will enjoy many bouquets when the London beaus discover your existence. It is preordained you will be a success." Recovering her poise, Mrs. Bell came close to grinning, her eyes twinkling: "Especially since *I* will have the dressing of you!" She sobered. "My dear child, you must not allow your education to interfere in your enjoyment of the Season. The one has nothing to do with the other. Allow yourself to dance and gossip and learn the art of the flirtation. That will not interfere with your ability to converse with the sensible people whom you will also meet, the politicians and writers, the artists and scientists. Scorn neither your Season nor your looks, child."

Impressed by this particular lecture in spite of herself, Georgi nodded. "Perhaps there is more to a Season than I'd thought. It has always appeared nothing more than a particularly objectionable shop where men, having decided it is time to wed, choose—sometimes very nearly at random—a woman they must meet at the altar before getting on with the begetting of an heir."

"But that is important, too," said Mrs. Bell with an airy gesture, "the begetting part. The unmarried lady is to be pitied."

Georgi, who very much expected to be one of that pitiful sort, found herself curious. "Why do you think so?"

Mrs. Bell's brows rose. "There is an aspect to marriage which is not allowed the unmarried lady. Ah," she said, when Georgi blushed, "you know of what I speak. Excellent. One hears of young girls kept in ignorance. Such flowers are particularly easy to pluck. The rakes and fortune hunters lead the innocent to disaster. I think you would give such a man a great deal of trouble, would you not?"

"Most definitely I would." Georgi gave in to her need for information. "But is that . . . aspect . . . so important?" she asked, hiding her embarrassment for fear the woman would think it improper to answer such a question.

"La! It is not at all important; it is merely enjoyable—

when engaged in with proper verve and élan, you understand, and not as a mere duty, as is the way too often taught to *tonish* girls." Mrs. Bell nodded. "I am educating you over and above what your grandfather would approve, am I not? Now it is time we discussed the reticules and hats and such. I will choose for you that which is needed for each costume, of course, but I wish you to understand *why* I choose what I do."

Georgi tried very hard to pay attention during her lecture, but found herself too often wondering if Lord Everhart would engage in *that* aspect of marriage with proper élan and verve. She was exceedingly glad when Mrs. Bell said they had accomplished all they could for one day.

"I will send to your hotel a hairdresser who will crop your hair and show your abigail ways to dress it properly." Mrs. Bell gave her an interested look. "You blush rosily. Now? When there is no reason? Why?"

"I have no abigail."

"Have you not? But you must have an abigail. Lord Tivington is remiss. I know a young woman who will satisfy. I will send *her* to you as well."

Somehow Georgi didn't have the courage to tell the modiste she'd done very well for nearly twenty years without such service and would prefer to continue in like manner. Obviously Mrs. Bell knew better, however, and Georgi found herself agreeing to hire the young woman. Then she found herself in a hackney carriage chaperoned by the gray-haired woman, who sat with her hands folded and eyes sternly forward.

Two days later, several new gowns in her possession, Georgi and her grandfather were once again in the coach and tooling down the Brighton road, followed by a second

carriage in which Grandfather's valet had been joined by
June Darwin, Georgi's abigail. "I've concluded," she said
firmly, "that I do not care for fittings and such."

"Is there an alternative?" he asked idly.

"I asked Mrs. Bell if it is possible to hire a woman
with my measurements to suffer in my place."

"And . . . ?"

"And she said she would try to find such a one before
we must begin my wardrobe for my Season." Georgi
chuckled.

"Something is funny? I have had a busy few days and
would like to laugh, my dear."

"It is only that old expression about clothing and the
man—in this case the *woman*. When the first evening
gown was fitted to me Mrs. Bell backed off, studied me
from all angles and, in an icy tone, asked how old I
might be."

"You told her."

"Of course I told her. She claimed she'd been led up
the garden path in such a way she could well have been
led to her own ruin." Georgi shook her head. "Would
you believe she has redesigned all my clothes simply
because she discovered I am nearly twenty and not a
chit of seventeen?"

"Redesigned them?"

"I exaggerate. The changes are subtle. Necklines a
trifle lower. Bodices just a trifle tighter. A touch more
color than she'd planned when choosing ribbons and
embroidery." Georgi shrugged, a trick she'd picked up
from Mrs. Bell. "She has forgiven me, my lord grandfather, but is angry with you and says she will have
words with you when next you come to town!"

"I presume it is that I am male and uneducated in
such things, but explain how she might be ruined by this
teapot-sized tempest."

"To dress a fully adult woman as a child? To fit me up as a wide-eyed innocent when, at the great age of twenty, I must have experienced enough of the world, even hidden away as I have been, that I cannot possibly maintain the appearance of naïveté? She would become a laughingstock, I am informed, for dressing ewe as lamb. She will not do it."

"I'd no intention that she do so and so I will tell her. It should be obvious to the meanest intelligence you are no child, Georgi."

"But it *isn't*. First, Lord Everhart and now Mrs. Bell, and there are no flies on that lady! She, at least, should have seen me for what I am."

"Do not wish yourself older, my dear," said her grandfather with a soft chuckle at her pouting face. "All too soon will you show age—although not so quickly, perhaps, as your cousin. You have good bones, my child, which will serve you well as the years add up."

Georgi didn't argue, but was growing tired of finding herself treated as one of the infantry when her grandfather had treated her as an adult from the age of fifteen when she'd first argued with him—that time on the idiocy of electing fools for seats in the Commons. "My age becomes a bore. Tell me, instead, what you have done while I've acquired a touch of polish?"

"I? Among other things," he said evasively, "I've been discovering what I can about your Mrs. Compton."

Georgi blinked. *"My* Mrs. Compton?"

"Hmm. I believe she will serve."

Georgi shook away the cobwebs that seemed to fill her mind. "Serve . . . ? Oh! *Serve*. I see . . ." She frowned. "I think."

"You see more than you should most of the time. Perhaps I'll tell you no more. What you do not know will not come to light by accident when it is least wanted."

"Yes," said Georgi promptly, "such a gabble-grinder as I am, you couldn't guess what I might let slip. Is she as rich as is said?"

"Compton cut up to the tune of more than half a million."

Georgi was so unladylike as to whistle, a talent she'd discovered upon losing a front tooth. "Surely that is enough to set the dibs in tune."

"My grandson is a ninnyhammer and a scatter-good, but gossip has it that his father discovered the whole before he'd quite ruined the family," said Tivington. "He has been given a good fright, actually spending a few days in the Fleet with other bankrupts before my son rescued him. He may be manageable if the touch is light *and* if it comes before he recovers from the shock."

"You've always had a good light touch with the reins," suggested Georgi.

"But it is not my hand which will hold them. Mrs. Compton has ambitions," Tivington continued. "She is also, as you informed me, a squeeze-penny, reluctant to step into a conventional marriage in which she would turn her fortune over into her husband's hands. Since she would like to put the stigma of her first marriage behind her by marrying back into the *ton,* I have bidden my solicitor draw up a marriage contract of a nature which she can approve. Or so is my hope."

"I thought I wasn't to know.

"You haven't heard a word, have you?" he scolded, frowning mightily. She chuckled as she was meant to do and Lord Tivington drew a traveling chess board from his pocket, told his granddaughter to stop rattling on like just any chattering minx, and to put her mind instead of her tongue to work. Georgi pertly informed her grandfather it was not *her* tongue which had run on. He again called her a minx, offered her white, and thereby, the option of beginning the game.

Georgi found Brighton interesting. She did not think she'd care to spend a great deal of time there, but she was not bored. Her grandfather, she discovered, was well known and well liked, regardless of the fact he'd not appeared in society for some years. Immediately it was known he was in town, invitations to various parties arrived. These included a dinner to be followed by a theater party and, wonder of wonders, an evening at the Pavilion. Lord Tivington accepted only those two, the first from his oldest friend and the second from Prinny, which, virtually a royal command, could not be turned down.

"You should not be attending either," said her grandfather mildly, "I will undoubtedly be scolded and nagged at for days by all three of your aunts when they discover I've taken a young lady not-yet-presented to the Pavilion. They can't complain about the theater, which is acceptable even if you are not out. I, however, do not think it will hurt you but I've explained you are not to be formally presented to our prince until next Season, so do not be chagrined if His Royal Highness ignores you. It should serve except with the highest of sticklers whom we do not care for in any case."

"We do not?"

"We will not allow them to dictate our behavior. I have never done so and I expect you to follow my lead, Georgi."

"But I've heard such horrible tales about how such very proper persons may ruin the Season of some green chit who puts a toe beyond the line."

"They won't ruin *yours*." Lord Tivington's glower intimidated an approaching inn servant so badly that the small tray he carried before him shook like a leaf. "What is this? A note? Very good, my man." Tivington gifted the

servant with a shilling, which soothed so well the servant
decided the old man might be a gnaggy old gadger but
was a right 'un nevertheless. "Aha! It is arranged so soon,
is it . . . ? What was that, Georgi? Oh. I am to *accidentally*
meet Mrs. Compton. I must leave you in our sitting room.
I know you wish to stroll along the promenade and see the
sights, but do nothing more to outrage your aunts, please.
My decision to give my head for washing, regarding the
invitations I've accepted, need *not* be considered an example you should follow. Please do not be tempted to go
out even with your new maid in tow. I am a reprehensible
old man to allow you the freedom you'll have while here,
but I would not like it if anything you did were to tumble
us into a true bumble broth. You will promise to await me
here?"

"I promise if you promise we may indulge in that
stroll when you return."

"It is a bargain. If all goes well, I should not be more
than an hour."

Evidently all went very well, because Tivington returned with a satisfied expression. Georgi was curious as
a cat as to what her grandfather had said to Mrs. Compton, but forgot it in the satisfaction of meeting several
great people who had, previously, been only names to her
and to whom she was introduced while out walking. Over
the next few days Georgi acquired several interesting new
acquaintances and decided that perhaps her introduction
to the *ton* would not be so bad after all.

Georgi and her grandfather returned to Beverly Place
in advance of their expected arrival. The first day all the
talk was of the boxes which had arrived decorated with
the name of the exceedingly famous Mrs. Bell. Lady
Melicent was not pleased to discover her niece had a
wardrobe from a shop she could not herself afford. Then
there was the new abigail. Why should she and her

daughter be required to share a maid and Georgi, who cared not at all for such things, have a well-trained London dresser? The new coiffure didn't please either. It gave a piquancy to Georgi's features which had been missing. In fact, thought Lady Melicent, the chit was growing indecently attractive.

Then a letter arrived from a friend in Brighton and Lady Melicent discovered Georgi had attended the theater. "Lady Axminster's party?" For years Lady Melicent had maneuvered, unsuccessfully, for an invitation to something more exclusive than one of the lady's annual squeezes. "How did that come about?" her chagrined aunt demanded of her niece.

"His lordship and Grandfather have known each other forever," said Georgi. "I believe they correspond regularly and his lordship must have dropped a hint of his wishes in his wife's ear, because the invitation awaited us when we arrived at our hotel."

"It is too much to hope you behaved in a properly maidenly fashion. The next we'll hear is that you've fallen into a scrape and we'll find ourselves beyond the pale."

"Prinny predicted I'd have a magnificent Season," said Georgi, stung. "He said he was quite taken with me."

"*Prince George* actually spoke to you?" Melicent gaped. "You were *presented?*"

"Not exactly." Georgi glanced around, wondering how she could have been such a gudgeon as to reveal exactly the information her grandfather had hoped to keep from her aunts. What a fool she was.

"How is one *not exactly* presented?" asked Melicent in icy tones, her eyes dangerously narrowed.

"One is a guest at the Pavilion," said Georgi, goaded beyond caring, "and one is talked to by one's host. He approved that I knew so much about Arthur Wellesley's temporary appointment to command in the Peninsula."

"You actually dared raise your voice in such exulted company?" Lady Melicent wondered if she might fake a swoon. The outrageous chit would take the shine out of Cassie if allowed to go on as she had begun. It must not be allowed!

Grandfather entered the salon in time to hear their last exchange. He sent a dagger glance toward his favorite, which was met by a remorseful look and one which begged him to save her from the situation in which she found herself. "Here's high flights," he said softly. "Why do I find a brangle in my drawing room?" His tone was that which, to the knowing, foreboded trouble.

Lady Melicent was too worried and suffering from such extremity of spleen she forgot her dependence on her father-in-law's goodwill and drove straight on. "You actually allowed your granddaughter to attend an evening party at the Pavilion." Her voice rose. "You are a fool."

"I may be a fool, but you are a shrew. I do not care for your tone, madam."

Lady Melicent might be a shrew but was *not* a fool. Her mind might be full of nothing but who was whom and what was what, but she knew what she knew full well. Cunning rather than quick of wit she went smoothly to the attack, using more tact than she wished, but doing her best to retrieve her position without damaging her purpose. "I should not have called you a fool for you can have no knowledge of what a terrible thing you have done . . ." She couldn't resist one tiny jab of spite: ". . . although you *should,* such a knowing one as you are! But the *damage* is immense. *She is not yet out.* She should not have been seen at the Pavilion and most certainly should not have bored on to His Royal Highness about things of which she can have no knowledge. She will have revealed herself as a hoyden and a bluestocking." Hoping she'd set the stage, Lady Melicent declaimed: "Georgianna Thomasina must retire from all contact with the *ton* until her unforgivable breach of manners is forgotten."

Lord Tivington spoke softly but with deadly intent. "We were invited by the Prince, who berated me for keeping such a lovely ornament away from society far too long. We were required to arrive at the Pavilion early so that His Royal Highness might have conversation with the chit when it would not be out of the way for him to do so. I am ordered to present her next spring at risk to health and wealth and perhaps my freedom if I do not."

The doors to the salon opened during this speech and Lord Everhart strolled in behind Brooks, who waited, properly, for a break in the conversation before announcing a guest. "You met Prinny, my child?" Everhart asked Georgi later when, with the arrival of more guests, conversation became general. "What did you make of him?"

"Charming and well informed about the war, which is more than can be said for many I met. But," she continued, her nose wrinkled in a thoughtful way, "for all that he studies the dispatches and is a avid supporter of the arts, it is my opinion he is bored. He is not young, but has been forced all his life to play second fiddle to his father. He's been allowed to do nothing of note while waiting for the old king to die so he may fulfill the role for which he was born. Yet one cannot be so unnatural a son as to wish a parent dead, can one? Such inner conflict must be terrible, turning the most easygoing of persons sour—and I suspect our prince was never of an easy temperament. I find it sad, yet I cannot condone how he *has* relieved his boredom, spending fortunes in architectural experiments and such oddities as forever designing new and expensive uniforms for his regiment."

"You are both stern and yet fair, I think," said Lord Everhart, wondering why she appeared older and more mature. The hair, he decided, and he complimented her on the new touch.

"Yes. It is a dead bore, but Mrs. Bell said it must be done or she would not allow me to wear the gowns she designed for me. I must own to discovering that I am no more immune to new clothes than the next woman. The process for getting them, however, is absurd and a dead bore!"

Everhart was pleased he'd discovered the secret of Georgi's seeming maturity: Mrs. Bell indeed! That woman could dress a flowergirl and make her look a lady, so it was no wonder Georgi looked older. He chuckled. Lady Melicent, hearing, gnashed her teeth.

Cassie sidled into the salon just then and was ordered, by a sharp movement of her mother's head, to join Georgi and Lord Everhart. Hiding her wish to do no such thing, Cassie dawdled as much as she dared, but since the salon was comfortable rather than awe-inspiring in size, she soon came up beside her cousin. "I have forgot my manners since you returned, cousin, and forgot to ask. Did you enjoy your travels?" she asked Georgi.

"Traveling is full of discomforts such as I never imagined. I believe I would enjoy Brighton in small doses, but London seemed a veritable fungus, as Cobbett has called it in his articles."

"You didn't like London?" Cassie couldn't imagine it. "You must be mistaken, Georgi. It is impossible to dislike London."

Georgi chuckled. "I will reserve judgment if you insist. It may be that the Season was over and I was there for only a short visit and could take no advantage of the things for which London is noted."

Everhart was more interested in her reference to Cobbett. "Surely you do not read his *Political Register*? He is a rabble rouser and—" He lowered his voice. "It has been whispered, a seditionist. He may very well find himself in Newgate even yet."

"Nonsense. The poor man is merely upset his world has changed from the delightful village life he knew as a child. He was happy then, so thinks it was something about the way the world was which caused it and not simply that any child in a well-run family is happy anywhere. But, as a result, he thinks that if we could return to that age, all would be perfect."

Everhart's brows quirked. "You do not agree it was a perfect age?"

"I doubt very much that there was *ever* a perfect era."

The discussion grew heated and Cassie grew bored. She hadn't a notion what Everhart and Georgi argued about. Golden ages? Government debt and taxes and the laborer? What did the working man have to do with taxes? It was all a jumble and made no sense. What a relief when Brooks announced dinner.

For once Cassie saw an opportunity in the shape of Everhart's arm and grabbed it. Fear of her mother as well as boredom made her quick off the mark. She hung on to him and there was no way he could avoid taking her in to the dining room. Since there were other guests this evening and the numbers were balanced, Everhart could not offer his other arm to Georgi, as he might in more informal circumstances. Their eyes met, his rueful, hers twinkling at his dilemma. Then she cast him an apologetic look and turned to accept the escort of a young neighbor. The young man colored up, the tips of his ears painfully red. He was embarrassed to find his old playmate looking fine as a sixpence and decidedly *unlike* how a mere *friend* should look.

Later, Cassie was asked to play the pianoforte to entertain the guests. Lord Everhart, by pretending not to hear Lady Melicent, managed to avoid turning the girl's pages. That prize position was occupied by another of the young guests, one among many who showed signs of being smitten with the English beauty of Lord Tivington's younger granddaughter.

Under cover of the music, Everhart asked Georgi about that last look she'd given him. "Before dinner? I was apologizing," she said after a moment's thought to recall the scene.

"For what?"

"For becoming so deeply involved in our discussion, which I am told by my aunts was most unbecoming to me, that I failed you."

"Ah. Our agreement. But I, too, missed Brook's announcement. If I had been more noticing I might have offered immediately to take you in. Besides, you failed me in no way. Our agreement was that I not be caught *alone* with the chit."

"Nevertheless, you suffered for four courses with Cassie beside you."

"On those occasions when I was required to converse with her I fell back on our old trick. I asked about my house guest and how he progressed."

"How is Sedgie?" A light flush touched her skin. "I should have asked, but so much has been happening I forgot."

Everhart glanced around. The other guests were politely attending to the music and paying the quietly conversing couple in the corner no attention. "I believe he can see again," he whispered.

"Didn't Cassie tell you one way or another?"

"*She* says she is exceedingly worried about him, that he is no better."

"Then why do *you* think he is?"

"I caught him looking in a mirror the other day."

"Why would he not inform . . . Oh."

"Yes. Oh. If he is well, then your cousin has no excuse to visit him."

"If he were well, we would invite him here. As an old friend of mine he'll be welcome to drop by as freely as you are."

"I'll tell him that."

"You might bring him on your next visit. Even if he can't see, it does not make him housebound. I don't know why he was not invited this evening. I will ask Aunt Marie."

"Perhaps you aunt doesn't wish to encourage *your* relationship with him." Ruefully, Everhart admitted to himself that *he* didn't wish to encourage it. In the world in which he lived it was impossible to imagine mere friendship between the genders. If gossip didn't ruin such attempts, then propinquity did.

"Encourage Sedgie? What can you mean?"

"You are not such an innocent as all that, child. You are growing up. She will not wish you testing your wings on someone so ineligible."

"But, *is* he ineligible?"

Everhart's eyelids fluttered slightly as he asked himself that same question. Sedgewycke was of a solid if not great family. He was, moreover, connected to a surprising number of families which were of the aristocracy. On the other hand, his sister had married a wealthy cit, presumably for his money, and one must assume the family was not well off.

"Georgi, I've no notion of his eligibility, but I'm certain he's not for *you*."

"No, of course not. He's for Cassie."

She missed his indrawn breath of relief. Relief for *what*, Everhart didn't know, and didn't wish to probe.

"That is, he is if he isn't beyond the pale," she continued. "Everhart, how may one discover such things?"

"You know he has not put himself beyond the bounds of polite society: He is invited to places where your cousin meets him." Everhart glanced up, and rose to his feet. "I'm sorry, Lady Marie. You wished to speak to me?"

"I wished to speak to my niece." Aunt Marie did everything but simper. "It is her turn to play for us."

"Is it indeed. May I turn your pages for you, Georgi?" he asked, holding his hand to help her rise.

"I play from memory, my lord. It will not be necessary to upset my Aunt Melicent more than we've done already. But I suggest you move quickly into my grandfather's orbit, if you wish to avoid a situation you say must be avoided."

Everhart turned to see Lady Melicent, Cassie in tow, bearing down on him. Deftly he removed to a chair beside his host. Georgi very nearly grinned at her aunt's chagrin. *Serves her right,* thought Georgi, seated at the pianoforte, her head bent in thought. She shouldn't make her intentions so obvious. Everhart was not one to be hunted but would, she thought, go hunting himself when the time came for him to choose bride.

The thought of that inevitable bride saddened Georgi. Her fingers, always slaves to her mood, chose to play a collection of mournful Scottish songs—all having to do with the loss, in a variety of sad ways, of a lover.

Seven

While returning cross-country from the village where Georgi had been on an errand for her Aunt Marie, a shout edged with panic broke into a daydream in which Everhart realized she was no longer a child and requested the right to make love to her with proper élan and verve. Jerked abruptly from the sublime to harsh reality, she stared up the long hill over which a heavy old traveling carriage had just pulled. A woman's terror-filled scream reached her ears. What . . . ? Ah! The drag, thrown out to slow the coach on the long downhill run, had broken loose and lay near the top of the overly steep slope. The horses would be overrun by the top-heavy and overloaded coach and an accident unavoidable.

Georgi's eyes narrowed, studying what might be done even as she urged her mare toward the disaster-in-the-making. A hidden lane angled off to a more gentle slope a little over halfway down the hill. Unless the driver knew the road he'd be unaware of it. So, if she could reach the team in time and turn them, she might save the situation. Georgi put her heel into her mare's side and leaned forward, encouraging the white horse to greater effort.

Reaching the runaways, she forced her mare close, reaching for a frightened animal's bit. She pulled. Suddenly, glowering over the horses' heads, Everhart was on the other side, leaning his heavier horse into the team from that side. She grinned, tugged harder, and the two of them, working together, turned the animals into the lane, where gradually, they came to a halt.

The coachman, red in the face, mopped sweat from his bald scalp with a huge red-figured handkerchief. "I thought we were a goner there," he whispered huskily. "Thankee. The both of 'ee. Thankee."

But Everhart was paying the man no heed. He'd come around the team, which stood trembling, heads hanging, and dismounting, pulled Georgi from her horse. He shook her. "Don't you ever try such a stunt ever again in your life," he yelled. "You fool. You idiot. You idiot chit, you have more hair than wit. A brainless peagoose would have more sense . . ." There was more of the same, a stiff shake punctuating each comment.

Georgi was too outraged by Everhart's reaction to speak—assuming she could have gotten a word out, since his shouting and the shaking were making it a trifle impossible to do more than catch her breath. She'd been set to indulge in mutual congratulations at a successfully accomplished maneuver. She didn't understand why he was behaving like a madman but was becoming more furious by the moment.

"You aren't listening to a word I'm saying," said Everhart. "Someone should teach you a lesson. Someone should beat the living daylights out of you and, if I were your grandfather I'd do just that." He shook her again. "Do you hear me? Do you?" Suddenly his hands trembled and he pulled her into his arms, pushing her head into his shoulder. "Damn you, Georgi, you could have been *killed.*"

"Let me go, you monster!" she gasped, her words muffled against his jacket. "You villain. You . . . you . . ." She could think of nothing bad enough until she recalled a French word Vincent had once used—one he'd refused to translate so she'd tucked it away in her mind, assuming it must be very bad. She said it.

Everhart pushed her away, his mouth agape, his eyes widened by disbelief. "Where in God's name did you learn *that?*"

Georgi blushed. "From Vincent. I haven't a notion what it means but it appears to have expressed my feelings."

"Thank heaven for small favors."

"Well?" She glowered. "What *does* it mean?"

"I'm damned if I'll add to an education which has obviously been far too liberal as it is," he said bitingly.

It suddenly occurred to him they were not alone. The coachman didn't bother him. That man was praying loudly and overly long in thanksgiving. The occupants of the coach, however, had helped each other out. One was a mousy-looking woman of indeterminate age. The other was Mrs. Alicia Compton.

"That's torn it," he muttered.

Worse was to occur. Lord Tivington, accompanied by Elliot, rode up. Elliot was laughing his head off. "Well, cousin, finally found someone who will curb your excesses, have you?"

"Your comments, Elliot, are neither welcome nor necessary," said Lord Tivington. "You will hold your tongue. Georgi, Lord Everhart went to extremes, perhaps, but he is correct in one sense. You are never to do such a thing again, do you hear me?"

"I am to see a coach going its merry way to inevitable disaster, and do *nothing?*"

"You could not know it would overturn. Besides, Lord Everhart could handle the team on his own. You did not have to place yourself in danger."

"When I reached the team I had no idea anyone else was near enough to help. I *had* to try."

Lord Everhart managed to bring his fear for her somewhat under control and did a turnabout. Through stiff lips, he said, "She is correct. Anyone with an ounce of courage who saw the problem would have done the same. I was out of line. I apologize, Georgi. You were—" He bowed. "—magnificent. Now, if you'll excuse me, I must be on my way. I've an appointment in Oxford for which I'll be late." He mounted and rode off.

"Cursed rum go," muttered Elliot, confused.

Lord Tivington, after a thoughtful glance after his lordship, turned toward the coach. "Mrs. Compton. You and your companion are unharmed?"

"Except my heart was in my throat and beating like I thought I'd burst, I suppose I'm not harmed. We're fine, now. Miss Beverly, I don't know what maggot got into Everhart's head, to treat you so. *I* think you wonderful."

"I believe," said Lord Tivington, "his fear for my granddaughter's safety led him to behave in a way he'll regret for some time. Anger is a not uncommon reaction when one fears deeply for another and one is relieved no harm has come to them."

"I believe that is true only if there is an affection involved," teased the woman, tossing her blond curls. She turned to Georgi. "You have made yourself a right conquest there, dearie. Everhart has long been the despair of matchmaking mamas."

Lord Tivington, noting his grandson's narrowing eyes, interrupted. "You have come because of my report of your brother's condition, have you not, Mrs. Compton? You will wish to carry on to the inn in the village."

"The inn?" Mrs. Compton looked blank. "I'm going to the Manor."

"The Manor? But, Mrs. Compton . . ."

"You told me my brother stays there?"

"Yes. But *you* may not. The inn . . ."

Only Georgi, seeking distraction from her anger at

Everhart—to say nothing of the odd fluttering feeling Mrs. Compton's words induced—noted Lord Tivington's satisfaction. She wondered what he was up to.

"It would not be proper for you to stay at the Manor," he repeated, his eyes flitting toward his granddaughter and back.

A mulish expression settled over Mrs. Compton's fine features, features marred only by a rather square chin, which hinted at firmness of character or, very likely, just plain stubbornness. "I will not stay at that poky little inn in the village. My brother will be chaperon enough and I will continue on to the Manor, Lord Tivington. I must see to my brother and how may I do so if I stay elsewhere?"

Besides, thought Georgi with just a touch of cynicism, the inn would cost, and if she were at the Manor as usual, it would be unnecessary to pay out any blunt. Georgi's eyes narrowed as she saw her grandfather shake his head. What *was* he up to?

"It will not do. *A bachelor establishment,* Mrs. Compton. The home of a man with whom you have no relationship but merely the most tenuous of connections."

"My brother . . ."

"Your brother thoughtlessly imposed on Lord Everhart's good nature and see what has come of it? Not that much has," he added, once again looking in a meaningful way toward Georgi. "I am told he improves daily. It will not be necessary for you to nurse him, my dear."

"I don't wish to stay in the village. I won't . . ."

"I believe there is a solution to the problem," interrupted Georgi. "Grandfather?"

"Yes, my dear?" asked her grandfather. His tone was innocent, but the look he gave her silently asked how it had taken so long for her tumble to what he wanted of her.

"I believe," she said, suppressing chuckles, "we

should invite Mrs. Compton and her companion to come to us. She may drive over to see her brother whenever she cares to do so, but it is true that he needs no nursing. If she stays with us, then the proprieties will be observed and she'll be far more comfortable than at the, er, poky little inn."

Georgi happened to look at her cousin and noted a sudden feral look. He nearly drooled while devouring, with his eyes, the delightfully plump figure of the little widow, whose blond curls, escaping from her bonnet, danced in the breeze. *Elliot's* plans for the widow obviously had nothing to do with marriage, but he was making them with no reference to his *grandfather's.* Georgi would put her money on Grandfather every time!

"Would you come to us, Mrs. Compton?" asked Georgi. "We have more than enough room and you are very welcome. I fear we are merely a staid family party, but you know the old saying about relatives needing leavening. Your presence will be a boon to us . . ." Especially, she thought, if you fall in with grandfather's notions and take dear Elliot off our hands.

The invitation was accepted and Georgi caught her mare. When she attempted to mount, she discovered her shoulders ached where Everhart had held her. She couldn't, much to her disgust, totally repress a gasp.

Tivington drew near. "Bad?"

"I can bear it," she said through gritted teeth.

"Very well." Lord Tivington turned to his grandson, who had approached Mrs. Compton and was setting about his goal of turning her up sweet, hopefully as sweet as widows were notoriously said to be. "George Elliot," he said, "you will immediately ride home and tell your Aunt Marie she is to expect guests. Georgi and I will accompany the coach."

The coach, at Lord Tivington's suggestion, ambled

along the lanes at an easy pace. There was always the possibility the axles or wheels had received strain during the near accident and should, his lordship insisted, be cosseted until they received a thorough check. Lord Tivington and Georgi walked their horses behind it.

"You had Lord Everhart in a tizzy, did you not?" Lord Tivington's eyes twinkled in that way they had, the one brow raised into an ironic arc.

"I certainly seem to have done something." She eased into a straighter posture. "Grandfather," she continued, a rosy glow in her face, "do you agree with what Mrs. Compton said?"

"That you have made a conquest?" He took pity on her when he noted how very embarrassed that suggestion made her. "If you refer to what she said about his having an affection for you, and therefore expressed fears for you by becoming angry, then yes, I think he likes you very well. You amuse him and make him laugh. He enjoys the arguments in which you indulge." Had the warning gotten through to her? Lord Tivington cast a glance toward Georgi, who stared straight ahead between her mare's ears. She had again lost a bit of her straight posture, but soon forced her spine into proper alignment. "I dislike casting the least rub in your way, Georgi, but I don't wish to see you fall into the dismals."

"Which you fear I will when he finishes at the Manor and leaves us in peace? It isn't as if I'd never see him again. He is, I understand from conversations with Cassie, very much an ornament of society."

"So you will cheerily wave him good-bye as he leaves and greet him again as a friend when you see him in town?"

"Of course." Georgi achieved a mulish expression which very nearly rivaled Mrs. Compton's talent in that direction. "What else?"

Lord Tivington forbore telling her. If she did *not* know what it was she felt for Everhart, then it wasn't wise to put the thought into her head. If she *did,* it wasn't kind to rub salt in the sore. They rode on in silence for the mile or so remaining before they reached home . . . where, gifted with Elliot's much-embellished story of Everhart's angry tirade and the vicious shaking Georgi had endured, Lady Melicent was, for once, all smiles.

Surely, thought Lady Melicent, no man who was the least enamored with a chit could yell such insults at her as her son had reported. Melicent was so much in charity with her niece, she forbore to object to the imposition of unexpected guests. Not that she had a right to object, since it was her father-in-law's home, but Lady Melicent might have done so anyway on the unadmitted grounds they didn't want still another well-looking woman around to distract Everhart from Cassie.

When Georgi suggested that Mrs. Compton would be welcome leavening for a purely family party, she hadn't realized how truly she'd spoken. Over the next few days Georgi was amazed at how smoothly the household went on. The only cloud on the horizon, to Georgi's way of thinking, was Elliot's dead-set at the widow. It was not the sort Grandfather had hoped. She diffidently mentioned her cousin's behavior one day when she and the widow were alone.

"Do not worry your sweet heart, dear," giggled their guest. "I've been pursued by the most dedicated of fortune hunters and most expert rakes since finding myself a rich widow. I've far more nous than to let that awkward whelp have so much as an inch—which he'd turn into a mile if he could."

"You dislike him?"

"He is an unformed cub—" Mrs. Compton tipped her head in thought. "—but has promise, I think." Her brows were lowered slightly, her eyes narrowed. There was a slightly pursed look to her lips, but the chin, that decidedly determined chin, was thrust more than a little forward.

Georgi cast their guest a speculative look. "What are you thinking, Mrs. Compton?" she demanded bluntly, as was her way.

The woman turned toward Georgi and noted her curiosity. Just as bluntly she said, "None of your business, child."

"Mrs. Compton," said Georgi slowly, "I wonder if I might help you."

"Help me? I've never yet needed help when such an unlicked cub is the problem. *You* are much too young to understand, of course, but I assure you, Elty is no challenge whatsoever. In fact, he may be that for which I've searched," she finished on a thoughtful note.

Irritated beyond measure by still another reference to what was believed to be her age, Georgi gritted her teeth in an effort to forbear ripping up at the woman. Mrs. Compton's last comment, however, went a long way toward easing that irritation, blanketing it with further speculation. "I am not such a slowtop as you seem to think. It is my belief Elliot wishes to give you a slip on the shoulder and do not say I should not speak of such things because if I don't we will get no further with this conversation."

Mrs. Compton's frown turned to a chuckle. "Not a slowtop but a minx?"

"Perhaps. Yet, if you have in mind what I hope you've got in mind, I still think I might help you."

"And just what do you think I've in mind?"

Georgi drew in a deep breath. "Mrs. Compton, may I speak freely?"

"Go right ahead, Miss Beverly. I much prefer plain

speaking to Lady Melicent's murky insinuations," said the widow, her voice dry as good bedding straw.

"I like you. I really think I like you," said Georgi, her tongue running away with her. "Do call me Georgi."

"I am Alicia. But that is *not*, I think, what you wished to say."

"No, what I wished to say, is that if you hope to trap Elliot into a marriage of convenience, then I'd very much like to have a hand in it."

Mrs. Compton blinked. "You'd approve adding me to the family? Are you aware I married a cit when barely out of the schoolroom and that I'm years older than Elty?"

"Just what he needs," said Georgi promptly. "Someone old enough to keep him in line."

Again that nice chuckle warmed Georgi. "I'm quite old enough to do *that* and *will*, if *half* what I've heard of the boy is true."

"Not *half*," said Georgi with a sigh, "but very likely *more* than you've heard! Oh dear, now that I've grown to like you, I don't think it *will* do to leg-shackle you to my harum-scarum cousin. He's wild to a fault, a gambler of the sort who never knows when to quit, and he's *mean*."

Mrs. Compton straightened up, and turned slowly to look at her young hostess. "What do you mean—now that you've grown to like me?"

Georgi sighed. "No flies on you, are there? I should never have allowed that to slip. Grandfather and I made a plan based on what we heard about you looking for a certain sort of marriage. We thought you might be just the person to take my cousin in hand. Or we had a plan. That is, *he* still does, of course, but I've got scruples. Now that I know you, you see."

The chuckles turned to deep, warm laughter. "What I see is that you are as flustered as a wet hen, something which doesn't happen to you all that often, or I miss my guess!"

"I've really muffed this conversation, have I not?"

"Georgi, I like you too. And I'll tell you straight-out it's in my mind to trap your cousin into marriage. I even know how to do it, but it will require just the right situation and just the right conversation. I'm going to have to work hard on that boy to bring him to a proper boil. I want a marriage where I can hold the reins and, if rumors concerning your cousin are true . . . ?"

"That he's under the hatches and in disgrace? Very true."

"Then I think I may put *my* plan into effect and reach an agreement where I retain control of my fortune."

"I believe that is exactly what Grandfather has in mind."

Mrs. Compton released a long breath on a whoosh of air. "That his lordship would not disapprove my goal eases my mind greatly. I had no wish to anger him, you see."

"Elliot's mother will not be gotten around so easily."

"At the moment she is pleased to have me here. I am a distraction for her son, one which will keep him amused and away from the gaming tables. I will deal with her when I have the right to do so."

Georgi digested that ruthless speech and nodded. "Alicia, may I ask an exceedingly impertinent question?"

"You can *ask*."

"But you make no promises about answering." They smiled at each other. "Will you tell me how you came to make your first marriage?"

A tension grew around Alicia's eyes, making her look more nearly her thirty years of age. "Everyone thinks I made that marriage for my Perry's money. It wasn't so, Georgi. I met him by accident when I was rather set on ruining myself and very much in need of a friend. He proved himself more than a friend and I fell deeply in love with him almost at once. It was mutual."

"He was a great deal older, was he not?"

"Not so much as all that. Eighteen years. But he wasn't to have a good life. We knew from the beginning how it would be so he set about teaching me how I should go on once widowed and how to handle my fortune." A tear fell and Alicia wiped it away. "I miss him. Even now. But I must keep to the plan we made to get me back into the *ton*. Perry said that's where I would be if it weren't for him selfishly taking me away from it." She shook her head, ruefully. "Georgi, a stubborn man with a guilty conscience is impossible to change. I never did convince him that the eleven years we had were worth it, even if I never do take that step back into society."

"Grandfather will help you, especially if you can keep a tight rein on Elliot. But perhaps you didn't understand when I said he was mean." Georgi described Elliot's behavior to his sister and told some stories from when all of them were much younger, how Elliot bullied everyone he could.

Alicia looked thoughtful. "Bullies are all the same, they back down if one stands up to them." She shrugged. "If it has gone further with him, which, from what I've seen of him, I doubt, I'll still have control of the monies. Any misbehavior on his part would be punished by a cut to his allowance." She grinned, her eyes glittering. "I'd enjoy cutting his allowance. I'm something of a pinchpenny, I'm told, always cutting corners and never casting my blunt away carelessly, but I'm aware I'll have to buy myself a proper husband. There is no way around *that*. I'll regret spending every penny of it, but I promised my Perry I'd be as generous as need be and I'll keep that promise."

"May I tell Grandfather that?"

"Hmmm? That I'm willing to buy a husband? You may if you wish, but add I'm not giving up control of my fortune for a gambling mad scrub like Elliot who would only play ducks and drakes with it."

"Grandfather wouldn't like that either. He'll wish to have a conversation with you before you go much further, just to see if your ideas match as well as he believes they will."

"You *are* a minx, but you must not mix yourself up in this one bit more than you have done. I'd prefer to handle Elliot my own way."

"Well . . ."

"Promise me."

"I will promise not to interfere unless it is absolutely necessary. There. The stable clock says it is time for luncheon. Shall we go in?"

They did. After her usual stint at piano and needle, Georgi hunted down her grandfather. She told him what she'd learned that morning. Lord Tivington grimaced. "Georgi, you might have ruined all."

"But I didn't. When she and Cassie return from the Manor shall I tell her you wish to speak with her?"

"That will not be necessary. Besides, you will have gotten so deeply into your writing you will not hear them arrive. I will give Booth orders to request her presence." Georgi glanced at her desk and blushed. "Don't take my words ill, child. I like it that you can concentrate so deeply you are impervious to the world around you. It is one sign of a well-disciplined mind."

"Or a selfish one which puts aside all else for her own pleasure!" She moved to her desk and, soon, was just as deeply into her work as her grandfather had predicted.

The one cloud on Georgi's horizon during the succeeding days was that she had no sight of Lord

Everhart. *Once again,* she thought, casting her line into yet another pool downstream from the mill, *I have set myself beyond the pale.* She frowned. Would she do anything differently if she were to witness another such situation? Georgi remembered the panicked look on the driver's face, the woman's scream. She recalled the frightened team. She would, she decided, behave in exactly the same way and *to the devil* with Lord Everhart . . . well, perhaps not to the devil, exactly, but why was the man avoiding her if not that she had disgraced herself in his eyes?

Georgi, tired of casting her line, allowed the fly to drift downstream. A bit later she was startled when someone sat on a boulder upstream. She discovered it was Everhart and her heart thumped wildly. "My lord?" she asked coolly after some minutes when he continued to stare across the water.

He turned slowly. "You are willing to speak to me?"

The brow Georgi didn't know could arch, arched halfway up her forehead. *"Me* speak to *you?* It is a question of you not speaking to me, is it not? I haven't seen you for a week and could only conclude you were avoiding me."

He smiled but there was a sadness somewhere behind it. "I didn't know how to apologize, Georgi. I'd no right to treat you so."

Georgi shrugged. "I was exceedingly angry at the time but Grandfather was pleased. Your scolding saved him the effort, you see."

Everhart relaxed a bit. "You are no longer angry with me?"

"I didn't say that. But only a little." She grimaced. "I was feeling so exhilarated by our success in heading off disaster. I expected to celebrate with you. You can see how I might have been more than a little surprised when you had other ideas entirely?"

He smiled. "We did do well, did we not?"

"We did."

"If you were a bit older I can think of several ways we might celebrate, all of which would be enjoyable." Georgi opened her mouth to tell him she *was* old enough but he went on before she could. "Since you are not, I have planned a dinner party which you and I will know is in honor of our success but will only seem a social evening to everyone else. I only waited to send out the invitations until I was certain you'd not refuse yours."

"I won't. You'll include our guests in your invitation?"

"Yes. I'll not forget them." He rolled his eyes up. "Actually I don't think I could if I wanted. Every time I turn around, there she is. She says it is because she feels *de trop* in her brother's room, where Miss Beverly reads to Aaron. She thinks her brother a slowtop since that is *all* that goes on, even when she gives him every opportunity to fix his interest."

"Fix his interest? Doesn't she know Cassie is already head over heels in love with him? Aunt Melicent thinks it is *you* my cousin goes all starry-eyed over when she drops off into a daydream, but I know better."

"Oh Lord, I'd forgotten that complication. Lady Melicent is still attempting to get the chit to attach me?"

"She assumes all is going on as well as might be— given those starry eyes I mentioned."

"Blast the woman. Will she never give up her ridiculous plans? I swear I will move to the antipodes to escape her and all matchmakers like her."

Georgi watched her line, preoccupied by the feeling something was nibbling at it. Absently, she said, "You should marry and put yourself out of their way."

"So I should. If the only woman I've yet met whom I

believe I could face over the breakfast cups year after year were available, then I'd think very seriously about making her an offer. Unfortunately—" He watched her concentrate on the line, thinking once again it a pity she was so young. "—it is out of the question."

He could not, he told himself, marry a chit who had never truly left the schoolroom; he believed, now, she was old enough to do so and wondered why Lord Tivington had not seen fit to give her her Season last year as—according to her aunts—should have been done. But then he recalled how Georgi had seemed a mere child to him when he'd first met her, seated up on the plinth of the Gabriel statue. Caught in an innocent prank, she'd patiently awaited her grandfather's return to help her out of it.

"Aha!" Georgi stood and pulled back on her pole, setting the hook.

Everhart stood, too, itching to take the rod from her hands, fearing she'd lose the magnificent trout rising and fighting and battling her every inch of the way. "Careful," he warned, reaching a hand around her from his position immediately behind.

"Don't you dare touch . . . !" She bit her lip, her eyes narrowing against the glitter and glare from the tumbling water. She coaxed the tiring fish another yard nearer, gave him a little line, fought him nearer still. "I think . . ."

"Careful . . ." he said again, this time more quietly.

"Perhaps . . ."

"Easy now . . ."

"Just a little more, you beauty," she breathed, and a moment later, reached down to catch the fish through the gill and lift it from the water.

"You've done it! Here! I'll do that for you. You can't like . . ."

"Nonsense," she interrupted. "Grandfather wouldn't have taught me at all if I'd shown the least sign of squeamishness." She removed the hook and, much to Everhart's surprise, knelt to release her catch into the stream. "It was a good fight, was it not?" she asked when she faced him and noted the look on his face.

"An excellent fight, but how will you prove your fish story when you've loosed the fish?"

"What fish story? You think I'd tell anyone what just happened?"

"You would not?"

"Good heavens *no*. In the first place I'm poaching—or I would be if I took the creature home. The fishing rights are *yours*, my lord," she explained when he looked blank. "In the second, if I were to tell about the size of that fish, not only would I be disbelieved, but, just in case there were something to it, we'd have everyone and his uncle's brother-in-law here trying to catch him."

He laughed. "But you will have competition, now I know what lurks in *my* stream. Worse for you, my dear child, I am not averse to eating my catch."

Georgi frowned, then sighed. "Well, he's a wily old devil and not often to be caught out like that. I think he'll be safe."

"Have you caught him before, then?"

"Once. A year or so ago. I've been trying ever since. You tell me you'll be here only for the hunting each year and riding to hounds will keep you far too occupied to catch old gentleman fish." She relaxed, having reasoned away her fears for her old adversary. "So, go right ahead and fish your stream, my lord . . . when you've time. I'll not object."

"Permission to fish my own stream, indeed! You are incorrigible."

"Perhaps." She looked up at him from under her lashes. "Are we friends again?"

"Were we ever not?"

"I thought I'd lost all your regard when you scolded me so."

"And I thought I'd made you so angry, you'd never forgive me."

They stared at each other and once again Lord Everhart felt that rising desire to draw her into his arms, to teach her the ways of passion. How *could* he feel so strongly about a girl barely of an age to join the husband hunting coterie that stalked London's ballrooms and salons each Season?

"There. You are doing it again." Georgi turned away to dismantle her rod for her return to the Place.

"Doing what?" asked Everhart when he was certain he had control of himself.

"Withdrawing from me. Going away somewhere in your head where I cannot follow and don't understand what it is you are thinking."

"And a very good thing you don't," he muttered.

"What?"

"Nothing, child."

"I do wish you'd not call me that."

"I should cast it into oblivion as I did the designation *brat?*" he asked, teasing her because he could not do what he wished to do.

"It deserves to be there. I am not a child, my lord."

"Are you not? I suppose you think yourself quite grown-up, but if you were, we could not meet this way. No, I think it best you remain a child as long as possibly you can. I would miss you if we were unable to talk and joke as we do."

Georgi's eyes widened. She had forgotten their meetings might be looked at askance. "Perhaps you are right, my lord."

"You agree with me? Will wonders never cease. But, I'm disappointed. I thought we'd have a nicely paced argument to end today's encounter, which would set up the both of us for the rest of the day."

She glanced toward the fully risen sun. "I fear I cannot oblige you. If I do not return home, at once, I'll not be there in time for breakfast."

Lord Everhart reached for her gear and, taking her elbow, helped her up the steep riverbank to where she'd left her mare. He tossed her into the saddle, liking the feel of her firm waist, which fit his hands to perfection. He forced himself to release her and handed up her fishing gear. "Will you be riding tomorrow?"

"I must make the rounds of our tenants tomorrow, my lord. Grandfather and I do so once a month and it is our day. The next day perhaps?"

"Blast. I am scheduled to go into Oxford again to see Sir Minnow's solicitor. I never knew how much niggling detail there was to settling an estate."

"Oxford? I have not been there for some time. It will be very pleasant now the students are mostly elsewhere!"

"You find the undergraduates a trifle wearing?" he asked with a grin.

"A *trifle?* My lord," she said, smiling down at him, "are you so ancient you have forgotten what you were like at that age?"

His smile faded, his eyes serious. "Georgi, those young men are just of an age to be proper suitors for your hand. Or they will be once you are out."

"I am a million years older than they, my lord. I think I'd best go, or we *will* have that argument for which you yearned and for which I insist we have not the time. Good day."

She turned and trotted off, increasing her pace to a canter when she reached the lane leading to the road home. Everhart watched her out of sight, before turning to stare at the stream. A surprising mixture, Georgi. One moment a minx, the next a siren, and yet again a laughing, joyful child . . . what did one do with such a one?

Marry her, said something deep inside him.

Everhart shook his head. He was over thirty and had no business looking seriously at a chit of sixteen or seventeen. If she were a mere ten years his junior it *might* answer, but he would not be accused by his friends of robbing a cradle.

All humor fled as he recalled how she felt under his hands, how much he wished to kiss her, caress her. . . . For long moments he berated himself for a fool. When he'd had enough of scolding himself, a rueful smile tipped the corners of his mouth.

You're blue-deviled my lord, said that voice in his head.

"Very," he answered, speaking aloud.

Eight

The invitation to dinner arrived later that day along with a note saying that Lord Everhart would bc in Oxford on Wednesday and were there errands he might run for the ladies? Lord Tivington read out the obliging offer during the evening meal.

"Oxford?" Lady Melicent's eyes narrowed. She glanced at her daughter and then at her plate.

Georgi could very nearly see the scheming going on in her aunt's head. She cleared her throat, drawing everyone's attention. "Grandfather, do you think Lord Everhart would object if a party were got up to go with him? I know he rides in to see Sir Minnow's solicitor, but that should not take him the whole of the day. I think Cassie has never explored the Oxford *backs,* and it has been a very long time since I strolled down St. Andrews, which is always worthy of one's attention. Perhaps a nuncheon could be bespoke for us at the Star and . . ."

"How you run on, Georgi," said her aunt waspishly, seeing her latest plot for entrapping Lord Everhart disintegrate. "You cannot think his lordship would wish to have such a number of people thrust upon him in such a way. Now, one or two, perhaps . . ."

"Lord Everhart has shown himself commendably amenable to falling in with the wishes of others," said Lord Tivington in a blighting tone. "I will call on him tomorrow while Georgi and I are out. I believe a day's trip into Oxford a very good notion and a little jollification just what we need. We have been too much in each other's pockets."

And so it was arranged. Lord Everhart, having met most of the local society by now, suggested others who might enjoy the treat, and notes were immediately sent and as quickly returned with positive responses. It was determined that such a trip would not set back Sedgewycke's recovery—assuming he were to ride in a carriage—and that he'd be happy to join the party. Plans were finalized very quickly and the younger guests set themselves to praying the next day would dawn bright and clear.

The revelers gathered at an early hour at the Manor, a variety of carriages and saddle horses attended by drivers and grooms crowding the forecourt. Alphonse was in his glory, overcoming all difficulties—about which he grumbled incessantly—to provide the company an excellent breakfast. The merry group set forth in good form, ready and willing to appreciate any and all diversions if one discounted Lady Melicent, who still regretted the plan she had concocted to, somehow, have her daughter stranded with Lord Everhart and, thereby, compromised.

One way and another it was taking forever for a marriage between them to come to fruition. Lady Melicent was growing more and more concerned. She could not stay forever with her father-in-law, indeed, did not wish to do so, since they agreed on very little and then only such unimportant things as that the Prince set a very bad example for the young men of the country. It didn't help, of course, that Everhart appeared to have taken one of those absurd, although always temporary, fancies men occasionally got for a chit like Georgianna Thomasina.

Lady Melicent looked forward to where Georgi and

Lord Everhart rode side by side. Something the chit said made him laugh, his head back, the sound ringing along the line of carriages to the one in which Melicent rode.

Melicent found it unbearable that a green girl like Georgi might capture hand and heart of such a man. Something *must* be done to discredit the chit. Georgi's unfond aunt had thought the near-accident which resulted in Lord Everhart's berating the girl would have done the trick, but somehow she had wormed her way back into his good graces.

Concentrating on ways and means to do her niece a disservice, she missed the details of her son's pursuit of Mrs. Compton, not that she'd have said a word about it. Considering the woman quite beyond the pale, Lady Melicent believed Mrs. Compton in no position to complain about whatever approach George Elliot might make to her, up to and including a slip on the shoulder. She didn't understand why her father-in-law had invited such a thruster into his home, unless, of course, he, too, wished to provide diversion for Elliot. It didn't occur to Lady Melicent that Lord Tivington would have been mortally insulted by the notion he'd turned procurer for his grandson.

Elliot rode beside the widow, glaring at any young buck who looked as if he might wish to make her acquaintance. Poor Elliot had found the widow blowing hot and blowing cold, and very nearly despaired of making her see the sense of an association that would be to their mutual benefit. In pursuit of those ends he reached for her hand and lifted it to his lips, very nearly unseating the both of them.

"You rudesby! Beware what you do," scolded his unloving widow, who had only moments before raised speaking eyes to him. It was enough to confuse the most knowing of men . . . which Elliot admitted, if only to himself, he was not. She chuckled. "You will be the ruin of me one way or another, will you not, my lord?"

Elliot, who commanded respect from no one, had never been called *my lord* before, and very much liked her doing so. He grinned in what he fondly believed a teasing leer. He hadn't a notion why his inamorata closed her eyes and quickly smoothed away an expression which, for a moment, he thought one of disgust. "Ruin you? Why, my dear, what sort of gentleman do you think me?"

"I don't believe I'll tell, my lord," she said, flattering him again by using the title and, thereby, once again, turning him up sweet.

"I wouldn't hurt a hair of your lovely head. I only wish—" Again he leered. "—*you* wished to put that head into my care?"

"Into your care, my lord?"

"Your head and, er, the rest of you as well."

Was this, she wondered, the moment? She looked around her, decided she couldn't run her rig so publicly, and ruefully decided it was neither the time nor the place. "You mustn't say such things . . . Elty, dear." Mrs. Compton wished she could force a blush. She put her heel to the side of her mare and it picked up speed, pulling ahead of Elliot. He attempted to catch her up, but another young man, seeing his chance, slid into place beside the widow Elliot bragged he'd bed and set up in a snug little house in Chelsea.

The young man had decided Elliot was much too sure of himself and began a flirtation in the hopes of bettering his own relationship with a widow Elliot swore was ripe and ready for all sorts of frivolity and jollification. . . .

The cavalcade reached Oxford in good time. Horses were left at the Star, where they would be rubbed down, fed, and rested for the return journey. Lord Everhart and Lord Tivington bespoke a large private parlor and, between them, in consultation with the inn's cook, chose a menu that would leave no one wishing for one more thing. Cold meats and roasted birds would be placed before assuredly hungry young people. Meat pies and fruit tarts would grace the table. Jellies and creams would tempt the ladies' more delicate palates. Good ale would satisfy thirsty men with wine, negus, and lemonade available for the women. Added to all that would be whatever fricassees and frumenties the inn's cook might dream up and have time to fix for side dishes.

That important point attended to, Lord Everhart took leave of his guests and disappeared toward the close in which Sir Minnow's solicitor had chambers. The rest consulted and broke into two groups. One wandered toward the famous Backs; Georgi joined the smaller group, which would study the plaster work of Thomas Roberts, which was illustrated by work in several Colleges' buildings. They went first to St. John's College's Senior Common Room, which was done in 1738, and then to All Souls College's Codrington Library, where it took Roberts fifteen months to do the Upper Library's ceiling.

Time was passing and the group docilely or, in some cases, with unseemly relief, agreed to only one more viewing, traipsing after Lady Bettindore, their expert and chaperon, toward Radcliffe Camera. There they cricked their necks to gaze at the ceiling on which Roberts cooperated with Giuseppe Artari and Charles Stanley. The graceful geometric pattern in which intricate six-sided figures decreased in size along eight "spokes" from the outer edge to the center was well worth a look. The wheel-shaped design was complemented by John Phillips's wood carving, the whole, they were told, having been done under the supervision of the great James Gibbs, who assembled the talented team—not that anyone was too interested in such facts.

Luncheon was the pleasant meal that had been expected. Everyone relaxed and joked and told of morning experiences if they could find someone from the second group who would listen. Lady Bettindore argued amiably with Lord Tivington as to whether the Radcliffe Camera Library was the better example of Roberts's work or if the Menagerie at Horton in Northamptonshire, which included the delightful Aesop's Fables medallions, should be considered so. After lunch, much of the party found it was rather unwilling to bestir itself.

Several couples, including Lord Everhart and Georgi, strolled toward the Thames. Lady Melicent immediately interrupted a conversation between her daughter and Sedgewycke and dragged Cassie off after them. She was determined that the day would not be a total waste.

The group by the river was feeding the swans bread left over from their meal. Lady Melicent immediately bemoaned the fact that she and Cassie had none. As she had expected, Lord Everhart handed over his. Lady Melicent then worried, loudly, that her beloved daughter not fall into the water and exhorted Lord Everhart to keep tight hold of her. Lady Melicent was a firm believer that physical contact led to immediate and irrevocable carnal yearnings on the part of any male between the ages of ten and ninety. She was certain that if only she could maneuver his lordship into holding Cassie by the waist, he would, without fail, fall victim to such urges. Lord Everhart, more wily than she wished, merely held Cassie's arm, keeping a firmer hand on Georgi, who was tossing chunks in a most unladylike way, wishing to reach the shier swans swimming beyond those pressing close to shore.

Something must be done. Georgi must be drawn from

Lord Everhart's orbit. It wasn't as if Everhart showed the least sign of being *enamored* of Georgi, but that, when she was there, he paid little or no attention to anyone else. Melicent schemed. When Lord Everhart announced he'd made special arrangements for everyone to view Trinity College Chapel, she recognized her chance. As the group strolled back toward the inn, where they were to collect the remainder of the party, Melicent stumbled and fell, allowing herself only a few regrets for the damage done her best driving dress. She closed her eyes and moaned.

The men conferred, wondering if they should carry her or look for a hurdle on which she might be placed. Lord Everhart, believing the lady to be shamming, suggested she not be moved at all, and that a doctor be found to attend her where she lay in case the situation was more desperate than they knew.

Melicent realized she was overdoing things and, with the help of a young neighbor, roused herself to a sitting position. "I am certain that with a little help I may proceed to the inn. I must not interfere with your little treat, however, and wish only to be settled in the parlor to await your return. Dear Georgi will keep me company while you visit the chapel."

Georgi's eyes widened. It had not, till that moment, occurred to her that her aunt was plotting to free Lord Everhart for Cassie's pursuit. "Of course, Aunt," she said, "if you truly wish it. I cannot think I'll be the least use to you, having no patience for the sickroom, but I'll do my best if you wish it of me." She encouraged the young men to make a rough seat with their hands, bullied her aunt into seating herself and placing her arms around the boys' necks to steady herself, and in general made a nuisance of herself organizing and ordering and causing a scene.

Knowing she'd brought the whole upon herself, Lady

Melicent glared. She told her niece, in hissing tones, not to make such an exhibition of herself, but Georgi refused to listen. Nearing the inn she hurried ahead of the rest and burst into the parlor, where her grandfather and another gentleman sipped a very nice hock. She urged her grandfather from his chair, talking loudly about the accident, about how her aunt wished her as her companion and how she must do her best to make her aunt comfortable. Melicent ground her teeth when finally seated in the chair and Georgi proceeded to require pillows and the preparation of a tisane and every other thing she could think of.

Finally she demanded: "Pastilles! I believe my Aunt Marie burns pastilles . . ."

Lady Melicent knew when she was beaten. If the amusement in her father-in-law's face were not enough, the worry in her daughter's countenance made it impossible for her to carry on. "I am not so badly hurt as all that, Georgi. I believe if everyone were to go along to the chapel and allow me to sit here quietly by myself, I will be quite recovered enough to travel home."

"But, Aunt, I would not wish to be remiss, to have it said I was lacking in sympathy or consideration for your poor shocked system . . ."

"Georgi," interrupted her grandfather, his tone amused in spite of himself, "Georgi, I have seen the chapel many times and would prefer to remain here until we return home." When she opened her mouth yet again, her face a picture of concern, he shook his head. "Run along," he said in a firm tone. "Think you I'm unable to care for ills such as your aunt has suffered?"

Georgi sent him a look brimming with laughter and her silent thanks for seeing through the ruse to separate herself from the party. She turned to Everhart, smiling up into his eyes and, with her back to her aunt, asked, "Do you think I may, with propriety, desert my aunt?"

"I believe your grandfather will see to her every need. Shall we go?" He held out his arm and led her into the hall and through the group of hovering guests. Everyone but Cassie followed. As the door closed, Georgi heard her cousin's clear voice: "I cannot leave you, Mother. What if the shock should suddenly retur—" The door closed on the remainder.

"Poor Cassie. What a scold she will receive this evening," said Georgi in an undertone. "I must await her in her bedchamber so that I may offer a shoulder."

Sedgewycke, who moved with much more assurance than one might expect of someone so newly blinded, overheard her. "Her mother will scold her for showing the proper loving sensitivities of a dutiful daughter?"

"For," said Georgi, her eyes brimming with laughter and her voice dry as dust, "*not* grabbing, with both hands, the opportunity to hang on Lord Everhart's arm, you looby!"

"It was a ruse?"

"A ruse to separate me from the party."

Sedgewycke glanced at Everhart, who pretended not to listen and was presenting an appropriately solemn mien. "From Everhart?" he hissed.

"Sedgie, you are not stupid." She and Sedgewycke slowed their pace. "My aunt, who has always looked down on me as a hoyden or, alternately, as a bluestocking, but, in either case, no competition for her Cassie, suddenly finds me monopolizing one of the more eligible prizes on the marriage mart and she cannot bear it. Lord Everhart has been chosen as a proper mate for Cassie, you see."

"How can her mother think of her and—" He flicked his eyes to the peer moving ahead of them. "—Everhart . . . ?"

"His lordship is not the wealthiest eligible, but he's the

most presentable and my aunt is not a totally heartless woman. The wealth, however, is far the more important. I believe her alternate choice was Mr. Davenant."

"That outsider?" Sedgie stopped in his tracks. "Are you serious she'd have agreed to a marriage between Cassie and . . . and . . ." Georgi nodded. Sedgewycke turned on his heel.

"Sedgie." He paused and looked over his shoulder. "You've changed your mind about quietly collecting memories and disappearing from her life?"

A muscle jumped in Sedgewycke's jaw. "I cannot bear the thought of it, Georgi," he said quietly. "And if that harridan would accept Davenant, she'll accept me."

Georgi strolled to where he impatiently awaited her. "It isn't generally known, but the family needs a generous settlement."

Sedgewycke came as close to sneering as he was able. "They'll get a larger one from me than from that hedgebird, Davenant." Again he turned.

"Wait a minute, Sedgie. Are you saying you are *rich?*"

He didn't stop, but turned and walked backward for a few paces, grinning at her. "Golden Ball has very little on me, Georgi. I wasn't poor to begin with and I seem to have the Midas touch. Everything I've invented has helped to make me richer."

"Do wait a moment!" Again Sedgewycke stopped. "Talk to Grandfather rather than my aunt. He'll be far less greedy and much more sensible. He'll also take Cassie's part, which my aunt might not do. She can be so stubborn when she takes a notion into her head." When Sedgie nodded agreement, Georgi turned and discovered her party disappearing on ahead, with Everhart about halfway between herself and the rest. He was looking from Georgi to the laughing crowd eager to reach the chapel and the treat he'd promised.

She lifted her skirts a trifle and ran lightly to catch him up. "Did you hear that?" she asked.

"Very little, but enough to guess at the rest. Have you sent him off to try his luck?"

"He'll at least have the sense to see Grandfather before talking to Aunt Melicent. I told him he should."

"Georgi, I hate to sound like a park saunterer puffing off his connections, but do you truly think Lady Melicent will take him in preference to myself?"

"She will once she finds the dibs are in tune."

"Georgi, wherever *do* you learn such cant phrases!" He sent her a look of pretended outrage. When she chuckled, he sobered. "Is it true?"

"He says so and it is something easily enough discovered if *not* true so why would he lie?"

Everhart drew in a deep breath and let it go. "Georgi, I begin to see the possibility of freedom from shackles! With any luck you will be out of a job very soon."

Georgi nearly stumbled, caught herself up, but was preoccupied during the whole of the tour of the chapel. Losing her special relationship with Everhart was a consequence she had not foreseen. Would she even *see* him if Lady Melicent was no longer in pursuit? Nonsense. Of course she would. But would they lose their easy friendship when he no longer needed her? *Oh dear . . . !* Such thoughts raced one after another through her aching head and she completely missed hearing the history of the beautiful Trinity College Chapel.

Sedgewycke reached the inn just as the door burst open and, blinded by sobs, Cassie rushed out. He caught her up and she struggled. "Cassie, Cassie, it is I," he said into her ear as he pulled her close. Instantly she ceased her attempts to free herself and looked up at him through tear-drenched eyes. "You are so beautiful," he added, his gaze flitting over her features. Cassie blushed and he grinned. "Come along, love. We'll walk by the river and you may tell me all about it."

"Oh! What did you call me?"

"My love."

"Mr. Sedgewycke, you mustn't say such things . . ." But, easily forgetting her distress, she blushed delightfully and peeped up at him from under long, fluttering, dark-tipped lashes with which she was an accomplished flirt.

"You'd prefer, *my dear?*" The blush fluctuated. "Or perhaps, *sweetings?*"

"Why are you teasing me . . ." Cassie stopped, pulled away from him, and when he turned a questioning look on her he found her looking quite pale.

"What is it, love?"

"Mr. Sedgewycke! Your eyes . . ."

It was his turn to flush. "I've been meaning to tell you, but—" He recalled the excuse Georgi had devised for him. "—I wished to be certain I wouldn't have a relapse. They've been improving all this last week."

"Then you won't be blind . . . ?"

"No. I believe my vision will be good as new very soon now."

"Then you won't need me to read to you." She pouted and looked down to where one dainty toe dug into the gravel path.

"I've enjoyed your reading very much, Cassie." He moved the few paces toward her and put his hands on her shoulders. She didn't look up. "I've enjoyed it so much, I wish it might continue for the rest of my life. I have a picture in my head. I see you sitting by a hearth, Cassie, with children at your feet. You are reading to them from a book open on your lap. And to me. I am sitting across from you with our youngest daughter on my lap."

Cassie looked up, her eyes again swimming in tears. "Oh if only it might be that way."

"You would like it?"

"Yes. But Mother would never allow . . ."

"If she will, will you marry me, Cassie?"

"Yes, please," said Cassie with great simplicity. "I'd like that very much."

"Do you think you could go into the parlor and ask your grandfather to come out to me? Or no," he added before she could respond. " 'Twould be better, I think, if I write him a note." He grinned. "Georgi thinks it better that I speak to *him* before facing your mother, my dear."

They strolled back to the inn, where the innkeeper supplied paper, pen, and ink. Cassie watched her Sedgewycke write a quick note, fold it, and giving it to her, close her hand over it. "Go now. The others will return all too soon and it would be best to have that talk here. Your mother will scold you for running out that way, but you needn't consider it. I do not like to suggest you should dissemble, but if you appear contrite, I'm sure she'll soon give over and give you some peace."

A few minutes later Lord Tivington strolled into the nearly empty taproom, discovered Sedgewycke at a table near the window, and joined him there. "You wished to speak with me?" Sedgewycke nodded. "About time, I'd say," grumbled Cassie's grandfather. "I expected you on my doorstep weeks ago."

Sedgewycke blinked. "You do not object to my wooing Miss Beverly?"

"Depends on *which* Miss Beverly. If it's my Georgi, then I think she has her eye elsewhere. But if it is that flighty miss, Georgette Cassandra, then, if you want her, *I'll* put no barriers in your way."

"But will you help us? Her mother will build moats

and walls and lock my poor Cassie away in the highest of towers."

"I am not doing this well, am I?" asked his lordship. "I suppose it is because it's been so long since Frederick asked for my youngest daughter's hand. The proper form is to ask about your circumstances."

Sedgewycke told him the bare bones of how his fortune was distributed between the 'Change and investments of other sorts.

Lord Tivington was so crude as to whistle. "That much, you think?"

"At least. I've not had an accounting for nearly a year now but have two new patents to my credit which will soon earn me still more income."

"I believe I'd not tell my son just where you've acquired your income. He'll be satisfied that you are willing to make a settlement. I suggest you offer no great amount . . ." Lord Tivington stroked his chin, thinking. "She is an earl's granddaughter, but that is no great thing and, besides, I have never believed children should be responsible for a father's irresponsibility, and my son *was* irresponsible in the way he raised George Elliot! Which reminds me, it is essential your engagement to Georgette Cassandra be kept secret for a time. I've plans," he added, noting Sedgewycke's brows raised to a questioning height, "which have not yet come to fruition. I'll tell you no more than that I need time. You must take Cassie aside and tell her the same thing, assuming you think her capable of keeping such a secret. If not, we will merely tell her you are going to visit her father to ask his permission. Then you will stay away until I inform you you may return."

Sedgewycke's grin was wry. "She has managed to keep it from her mother that it is I she visits at the Manor and that, very often, she never so much as sees Lord Everhart.

I think the visits would have ceased long ago if Lady Melicent had been aware of the true situation."

"So. The chit isn't quite the block I thought. Hmmm." Again thumb and finger pinched and rubbed the old chin. "Sir, I still think we must keep her in ignorance."

"I fear," said Sedgewycke quietly, "that, despairing of any chance we might come about, she will fall in with her mother's plotting and allow herself to be bullied into trapping poor Everhart."

Tivington nodded. "Now you point it out, I agree that is possible. I am so used to Georgi, who has a mind of her own, that it hadn't occurred to me most young ladies can be bludgeoned into doing as they are told." He shook his head. "Well. I suppose something must be said to her. Perhaps that you have gone to her father *with my blessing,* and that I feel confident we may soon *wish her happy?*"

"But that, even so, it must be kept from her mother . . . ?" asked Sedgewycke. Tivington nodded. "How intriguing."

A waiter approached their table with a message. Lady Melicent was tired and not feeling well and required that their carriage be brought around so that she might go home. At once. Lord Tivington's brow rose. "The woman is a shrew. I told my son how it would be when she first caught his eye. I knew her mother and her grandmother and I was right, was I not? I wonder if it has occurred to her she will discommode the two young ladies who rode in with her. They must be squeezed into someone else's rig if she leaves. Inconsiderate and selfish! Georgette Cassandra seems to have missed the taint, but George Elliot has it in full measure." He sighed. "Can I stall her, I wonder, until the others return. . . . I think I can. Excuse me."

He was successful. He also helped Cassie squeeze into a neighbor's barouche for the return journey. That

Sedgewycke was taken up by that same carriage was not the reason he gave Lady Melicent for changing her from theirs to the other. He said he wished Georgette Cassandra to become better acquainted with the neighbor's daughter, who had told him how much she liked Cassie.

Cassie gave her grandfather a look brimming with her thanks which he hoped his daughter-in-law had not noticed. But since Lady Melicent didn't consider Sedgewycke eligible, and believed her daughter no longer interested in him, she'd not particularly noticed *anything* about him, including the fact he seemed to know her daughter far better than she would like.

While driving, the young lovers could have no private conversation, but once they arrived at the Manor for another luscious meal prepared by Everhart's French chef, Sedgewycke positioned himself to help her out of the carriage. He whispered, "Have faith, Cassie. We have hope. Your grandfather will support us, but, because your mother will not approve, it must be kept a secret until I've seen your father and have his consent. Will you trust me?" She nodded, her eyes shining. "Then keep silent about us, or, at most, talk only to Lord Tivington, who favors us. I'll leave tomorrow and return when I can. My blindness made me forget a couple of obligations which have been put off far too long," he added, since he feared it might be some time before Lord Tivington gave him the nod and he could return. "So that I will not have to leave you once we are officially engaged I will take care of those little problems now while I am gone. Do not be concerned if that is longer than you like, my love. I am quite sure all will come out in the end as we wish it to do. Have faith, my love."

Once again Cassie's eyes glittered with an excess of moisture, but she only squeezed his hands meaningfully, smiled, and whispered that she understood how important it was that her mother not guess. Much to Sedgewycke's rueful amusement, she allowed another young man to take her around the house to the terrace, where the alfresco meal was laid out on trestle tables. Her grandfather, he thought, would find such deviousness another surprising sign that his granddaughter was not quite the ninnyhammer he'd believed.

While Cassie's hopes were rising that she might, after all, find happiness and fulfillment with her own true love, her brother was finding the progress of his plans more confusing than ever. The widow had not only *not* come to terms with him, she had actually had the gall to contradict him when he'd offered up his theories concerning play and pay. Who was she to tell him it was nonsense that the luck would turn if one only persisted long enough or to insist the nag one depended on to get one out of the suds was *always* the one who cast a shoe or stumbled on the turn?

She also said it was only good business that the house should win if one played at a hell. Why else, she'd asked, should they stay in business if it were not to make a profit? He'd had no answer to her innocent question and had, he recalled with bitterness, blustered and browbeat her until she'd given him a look which suggested extreme disappointment in him and wandered off.

And that had hurt. But why should he care what she felt for him, anyway? What was wrong with him that he resented seeing that ass, Robby, the Reeves twins' oldest brother, help her choose her food? Elliot decided the party had gone flat and ordered up his horse. Play second fiddle to a long drink of water like Robby? A man who didn't know one card from another? Never. If she preferred a gangling scarecrow who wore coats he could shrug into and waistcoats so conservatively styled they might have been worn by a vicar, then she could forget any offer from him to set her up in a nice little house in Chelsea. He wouldn't do it . . . not if she were going to go off in a snit for no reason and leave him looking a fool before the friends to whom he'd bragged so loudly.

Halfway back to Beverly Place it occurred to him the family was not expected and there'd be no dinner for him. Immediately he turned aside and headed toward the village. He wondered where he might find entertainment. A cockfight or a battle in the rat pit would be nice, but he'd settle for the charms of the barmaid if nothing else was available.

He pictured the barmaid's lush figure and, much to his surprise, didn't find it particularly appealing. Bah. Women. Perhaps he'd cry off the species altogether. He'd never met one, except perhaps his mother, who understood him. Even his mother had been shocked when she discovered he'd had to be bought out of the Fleet and horrified when she'd discovered to what tune his father had had to lay down his blunt. In fact, for the first time since he could remember, she'd been angry with him. His *mother*. Life was hard, thought Elliot, and women a tool of the devil.

Then Elliot remembered flirty eyes and golden curls and a husky voice calling him Elty. He sighed. Deeply. Women might be the devil's invention, but, if so, somehow the devil had found the key to a man's ruin. In the morning, he decided, he'd send her a poesy with her morning chocolate and apologize for his rudeness. Perhaps he could worm himself back into Mrs. Compton's good graces. He was almost sure she liked him. But perhaps not. If she liked him she'd be like his mother and not contradict him or try to change him. Oh fiddle. He'd never understand them and that was a fact . . . which didn't, unfortunately, make the dear creatures less necessary to a man.

At the inn there was a decent rabbit stew to be had and an excellent beef and kidney pie, to say nothing of a well-aged cheese and a good burgundy. A very good burgundy. *So* good he had a second bottle. Dinner finished, Elliot felt much more mellow—until he discovered his purse had been pinched so that he could not place a bet as to which of the dogs would kill the most rats in the given time. He was so irritated by that and so fuzzy from the wine, he very nearly felt it a good joke he'd allowed himself to be rooked, his pocket cleaned of not only purse, but handkerchief and penknife as well.

He would have been shocked into sobriety, however, if he'd had the means to discover his would-be inamorata in conversation with her groom. The groom turned over three small items to Mrs. Compton, received a reluctantly proffered guinea in return, and both felt themselves very well satisfied by the evening's business. Mrs. Compton had discovered a sure means to see her future spouse not bet beyond his means—that is, she thought so until she recalled it was possible a man might write vowels for the purpose. Well, she sighed, she'd never particularly enjoyed having an easy solution to a problem. She'd just have to think again, wouldn't she?

Nine

Georgi threw a stone into the deep pool where her old friend, Sir Trout, lived. About to throw another, a touch of guilt stopped her. Why shatter the old fish's peace just because she felt her world was on the verge of disintegrating? The trout was innocent of any fault. So, for that matter, was her grandfather, the deus ex machina of her problem. So, too, was Lord Everhart, who had never asked anything of her but friendship. Nor was it Cassie's fault; the poor girl could not be blamed for her mother's ambitions. In fact, it wasn't even Aunt Melicent's fault. Aunt Melicent had known nothing of the type of man who would rouse Georgi's untested emotions. She had chosen to pursue Lord Everhart for Cassie long before Georgi met the man.

Georgi tried to skip a nice flat stone, but the moving water was not still enough and the stone sunk without once rising. No, she had nobody but herself to blame for the loss of her ridiculous heart to a man who persisted, willfully, in treating her as if she were still in the schoolroom.

Very likely, thought Georgi, deep into self-pity, *he does it calculatedly. I am no danger to him so long as he behaves in ways which might not be misconstrued — and how can one misconstrue such an avuncular manner as that of Lord Everhart?* Georgi threw another

stone, hard—this time across the river and onto the far
bank.

"Something upset you, Georgi?" asked Everhart from
the bank above her.

Georgi froze. Then she twisted to look up at him. "I
didn't hear you approach."

"I tied my horse in the middle of a good piece of
grazing and walked." He half jumped, half slid down the
bank to where she stood near the streambed and bent
down to dust off his boots. "You didn't say what had
upset you."

Georgi managed to gain control of her emotions
while he rubbed his handkerchief over the toes. "A
small tiff. Nothing to signify." He tipped his head, his
brows rising as if he didn't believe her. "Really." After
all, it *was* no more than a tempest in a teapot, this argument she was having with herself. Every young woman
fell in love at least once before making an appropriate
marriage, or so her Aunt Marie insisted. She merely had
to get over her first infatuation, belated as it was, so that
she could get on to the next one. Didn't she?

"Now what does that look mean?"

Georgi blushed. "I was wool-gathering, that's all. I
didn't mean to stare so rudely."

"I'm beginning to feel a trifle out of sorts myself," he
said slowly. "I thought we were friends, young Georgi."

"Are we not, then?"

"Friends share their troubles."

"In our case that would be a trifle one-sided, would it
not? I mean," she said when he frowned, "I may have
my little problems and I'm sure you have experience
enough to suggest cures for them, but what value would
my opinion have in the solving of what must be the far
more complicated worries which might beset you?"

"Are we to have a theoretical discussion in order that

you may avoid telling me what it is that bothers you?" he asked politely.

Georgi glowered. "If you are perceptive enough to ask that, surely you are perceptive enough to realize you *needn't?* Following my lead, you could not probe where you are not wanted."

Everhart straightened, his back stiffening. "I see."

Georgi rose to stand before him, a sudden fear that she'd driven him off with her surly comment giving her insides a twist. "I didn't mean that. Not the way it sounded. It is just that I am embarrassed and don't know *how* to talk about my problem, which is not one which has a solution satisfactory to me. I will come about, my lord. Truly I will." When he didn't say anything and, worse, didn't relax, she held out her hand to him. *"Please* say you forgive me . . ." Oh, feathers! Even she could hear the desperation in her voice. What would he think *now?*

What he thought he didn't immediately say, but he relaxed and, with a gesture, suggested they seat themselves. It was his turn to toss small pebbles into the water. He did so absently while thinking. "Georgi," he asked, sympathy strong in his tone, "is it that your feelings for Sedgewycke were stronger than you wished me to believe and you are upset he has gone off to seek Miss Beverly's father's permission to approach her? If it is that," he went on, "it is no help to say you will get over it soon enough, but true for all that. You are young and you will find, more than once, perhaps, that you are attracted to some man who, very likely, does not return your affections. It is the way of the world." He chuckled, a self-derisory sound. "I remember my first infatuation. I must have been about your age, or perhaps a little older. I think I was all of eighteen—"

Eighteen? He thought her younger than eighteen! She'd known he was mistaken in her age but this was ridiculous!

"—and the woman was a friend of my older sister's. I was distraught for all of one Season when I discovered she was, even as I met her, on the verge of contracting a very good marriage. At first I dreamed that perhaps I might rescue her from the ogre who had dared raise his eyes to my princess, and that she might be so appreciative of my rescue she'd immediately fall deeply in love with me. As it turned out, she loved and was beloved by her fiancé. I dared suggest a wild plan to carry her off to the border where we could be wed over the anvil and then live quite out of society, which, of course, would shun us for such outré behavior. I told her we'd never more set eyes on the villain who would surely treat her badly if she were forced to marry him. She *laughed* at me." Everhart shook his head. "I was soon over my infatuation after that treatment, I can tell you. But there followed an opera dancer who took my eye. I was still very young and very idealistic and she a canny lady but she accepted a large sum of money to salve her broken heart and loss of title when my father pointed out to her the snubs she'd endure if she were to press me to keep my word to marry her." Everhart sighed. "We are such fools when young, Georgi. I swear to you that however painfully you feel Aaron's rejection, you will soon enough forget it."

Georgi bit her lip. It was the answer to her pride, wasn't it? Allowing him to believe what he chose to believe? And wasn't there a possibility he was shamming it? That he knew her silly heart beat more rapidly when he was near, that her blood heated at his merest touch, and that a wild fantasy of a future with him set her mind in a tizzy? In that case he was very kindly allowing her to keep her pride in the face of his lack of returned affection. She sighed. "My aunt has told me the same thing, my lord. Was your opera dancer very beautiful?"

A flush reddened Everhart's ears. "Georgi! What will

you ask next? But it is my fault, is it not? I should not have mentioned her, except that I was carried away by a touch of nostalgia. You will oblige me and forget I said such a thing to you."

"Cousin Vincent is always telling me about his bits of muslin."

"Cousin Vincent should be horsewhipped. It is an outrage!"

"Cousin Vincent," said a new voice, dry and with just an edge of danger, "is *more* outraged by finding his cousin alone with an adult male not of her family! Well, brat? Should I call him out and pink him royally or should I defend your honor by milling him down and spilling his claret?"

Georgi, at his first words, stood and swung around, a welcoming look brightening her features. "Vincent! You've come!"

"I wrote you I'd come, my unbelieving brat. You will, eventually, learn that I keep my promises. To you, at least. Well, Everhart? What explanation do you give for being here alone with my innocent cousin?"

"Georgi and I are friends, Beverly. You have no reason to object to anything that has passed between us this summer. Actually, Georgi has been doing me a favor and protecting me from your Aunt Melicent's plots to trap me for your cousin Cassie."

Vincent grinned. "I hear from Grandfather that you'll need that protection very little longer. Brat? Do you approve of Cassie's choice?"

"Why do you ask me? You know Sedgie. You and he used to be friends. Good friends."

"We still are although we no longer see so much of each other. I had hoped to speak with him before he left to lay his case before my uncle but he has gone already." Vincent, his young, dark, somewhat dissipated features set off by a carelessly tied cravat and windblown mass of curly hair, dropped down beside them. "Have you caught Sir Trout recently?" he asked, a speculative stare probing the pool where the fish could usually be found.

"She's done so at least once," said Everhart. "I was here when she hooked him and you don't know the difficulty I had not taking the rod from her so that I might bring him in myself. I was certain she'd lose him."

"I can imagine it very well. I can also," he added in that dry tone which stained so much of Vincent's talk, "imagine your shock when she let him go." Everhart nodded. "I'll have to have a go at him myself. Georgi, what is this about marrying Elliot off to that piece of dirty linen I found visiting?"

"If you mean Mrs. Compton, Vincent, say so. You know *her* full well, too," scolded Georgi. "Why didn't I meet her when we were younger? I like her. In fact, I like her very nearly too much to see her married to Elliot!"

"She's a right vulgar little piece of . . ." Vincent raised his hand, when Everhart would have stopped him in midstream. "I assure you, Everhart, she knows all the proper words. I probably shouldn't have taught them to her, but I was rather young and full of myself at the time and since she knows them now anyway, I see no reason to pretend she does not. But if it offends *your* sensibilities, I will do no more than ask Georgi for an explanation of why we are promoting such a connection."

Georgi tried to remember if Everhart knew of Elliot's deep doings at turf and table. She decided it didn't make any difference. "I don't suppose you knew our cousin spent some days in the Fleet recently?"

"Oh did I *not!* He touched me for a loan to tide him over. *Me.* I wonder where he got the notion I'd loan him anything even if I had had the blunt available. Elliot has never been my best friend—not quite my worst enemy, of course, but very nearly!"

"I presume he was desperate," soothed Georgi. "In any case, Uncle pulled his coals out of the fire, but has cut his allowance and is ordering his life for him, saying he'll not allow his son to bring an abbey to a meg—at least not while *he's* above ground, he won't."

"Which explains why our dear cousin is here this summer instead of preening it along the Styne. But it still doesn't explain the Golden Widow."

"Of course it does. She is very rich."

"And you think she'll frank his little games? You know nothing about her, if you think that."

"We *don't* think it. She'll retain control of her fortune, and she'll control Elliot through it."

"Georgi . . ." Vincent rubbed his chin very much in the fashion Grandfather did when thinking. "Georgi, I don't quite know how to say this so you'll understand, and so Everhart here won't jump on me for using vocabulary unbecoming to your ears, but Elliot is not exactly known for his patience and is not the soul of kindness—especially when thwarted."

"That worried me too," Georgi agreed. "Alicia seems certain she can control him. She even says he's not such a bad boy as he seems, but only in need of a bit of affection and affectionate guidance." Georgi studied Vincent's hardened features. She moved closer and touched his arm. "You see, don't you, that such a marriage *will* do for Elliot?"

"What I see is that the family will become a laughingstock." He compressed his lips when Georgi tipped her head, that brow she didn't know arched, arching very nicely. "Has it occurred to you, brat, that, much as one hates thinking of a world without him, Grandfather cannot live forever. Nor will our uncle. If they wed, that vulgar woman will, one day, become Countess? Can't you see her redecorating the Place with . . . oh, hand-painted oriental wallpaper and dragon-shaped chandeliers and carved screens and . . . *I* don't know." Pain colored his voice, a revelation he'd have descried if he'd known of it. "A sacrilege, Georgi. The Place is perfection just as it is."

Georgi was touched by the note of desperation. She glanced at Everhart and saw understanding and sympathy. For the first time Georgi had a glimpse of how deeply Vincent loved Beverly Place, how much he must resent it that Elliot, who had never liked it, must, someday, inherit it. *Too bad,* she thought, *that Vincent is not just a touch more dishonorable than he's said to be! He might find a way to save the family from that eventuality.* Then she scolded herself for thinking something so terrible.

"She won't, you know, not the vulgar and very Golden Widow," said Everhart. Recovering his countenance at the humor in that, Vincent asked how Everhart could know. "According to her brother, she's cheeseparing with her blunt if not downright miserly and has a commoner's dislike of waste. She will not replace perfectly good furniture simply to be in style so that is one worry you won't have."

Vincent nodded. "There is nothing to be done about it in any case. I will admit I hoped Elliot might catch a nice virulent case of jail fever while languishing in the Fleet, and would oblige me by allowing it to carry him off, but he has never been an obliging soul. What cannot be changed, must be endured. Although I find my cousin Elliot one of the more difficult things I am required to swallow in this badly arranged world in which we live. Georgi, I was to tell you you are expected home immediately."

Georgi stamped her foot. "You have been nattering

away forever when you had a message for me? Vincent, you are impossible."

"Of course. I would not be me, were I not. Come along, brat. I'll give you a hand up onto your mare's back and then, perhaps, Lord Everhart will join me at the village inn. I'll stand you a pint or two of old Potter's best, my lord, and a plate of the day's ordinary, which should hold us over to dinner."

"I'll gladly join you. Come along, Georgi. If your grandfather wishes you home, you'd better be off."

"Oh, not *Grandfather*. Our Aunt Melicent. I believe our aunt has become suspicious of where you go and what you do when you are out for hours. *Without a groom,* too, I'm told. Why Georgi!" Wide-eyed, he pretended outrage. "How *could* you, my dear?"

"Very easily. I don't suppose you'd spring for three plates at the inn? No? I thought not. Fiddle. Well, I will not return home at *her* demand. You may tell my aunt that you did not find me and that you had luncheon with Everhart. That will throw her off the scent."

"If you will not go home, where will you go?" asked Everhart.

"It has been some time since I visited my old nurse. I will do so. Vincent, if I am late home, do tell Grandfather where I've gone, will you? Nanny so hates to see me go until I've told her *all* the gossip. The family has always been her whole life."

"I'm to be your errand boy, then? But I know you like Nanny's way with cheese toast which she will insist on feeding you so you likely *will* be late. Very well, brat. Come along now, so I may put you up."

Everhart and Vincent watched her splash through the ford and cantor off in the direction of Nanny's cottage before mounting and riding in a nearly opposite direction toward the village. The bird was good. A pigeon pie was truly excellent. The home brew was something more than tolerable and the two men withdrew from the common room to the small garden behind the inn with a second pint.

"This is very pleasant. I was unaware of its existence."

Vincent shrugged. "Not many are. Old Potter doesn't allow just anyone to enjoy his private garden."

"He evidently likes you."

"Yes. I saved his son a drubbing once when Elliot was angry with him. I've been in Potter's good books ever since."

"Must have been some time ago, surely."

"Oh, ages and ages. Do let us talk of something interesting." Vincent looked over the brim of his mug, eyeing his guest speculatively. "Such as Georgi."

Everhart chuckled "Protective bantam, are you not? Don't worry your head. Little Georgi is suffering her first infatuation as we all must, but she'll recover."

"You say that," said Vincent, an edge of anger biting off his words, "as if you find humor in the situation."

"I'm not laughing at Georgi. I was, again, thinking of the ass I made of myself during *my* first brush with the more tender emotions. Or my second or third for that matter. I was explaining to the child she would recover when you arrived."

"I suppose," said Vincent, not quite knowing what to make of the man, "you find it gratifying."

"Gratifying? What would I find grat . . . Oh. You mean that Georgi will listen to my advice? She's a bright child. I like her."

"You persist in calling her a child."

Everhart chuckled. "I find I am jealous that you may call her brat. I'm not allowed to do so. It was part of our agreement that I not."

What agreement? wondered Vincent. "I've called her brat since she was six and I was nine and we spent my vacations getting into trouble."

Everhart, no slowtop, froze. "You look to be about twenty-five."

"I don't know if that is compliment or insult. I am twenty-three."

The rigidity which had stiffened Everhart didn't relax. "I see."

"You thought her younger? Then I'm not sure you do see. Not if you think *Georgi* planned a trap, getting you for herself, instead of for Cassie."

"I have spent hours with your cousin this summer. Alone with her. She has been compromised in theory although *not* in fact."

"You have treated her with the careless camaraderie you would a well-educated and intelligent youth. I know." Vincent waved a hand. "I've no intention of accusing you of compromising my cousin. But I canceled more than one interesting invitation and disappointed several friends who were counting on me so that I might come to the Place at this time. Georgi's letters have been full of you, my lord."

"I presume that is because I'm a new arrival. Surely they have also been full of Aaron Sedgewycke."

"Sedgie? Why?"

"I have suspected it for some time although, when I first asked her, she denied it. Today I found her unhappily tossing rocks at the water and challenged her with it again. She didn't deny it." Everhart frowned. "On the other hand, she didn't confirm it either. Now I know her age, I fear her affections may go deeper than the childish infatuation I'd thought it . . . Poor girl. How gallant she is to have promoted her cousin's interests as she has this summer!"

Vincent, who had followed this with some difficulty, began to see the light with the last words. "Let me see if I understand this. You believe Georgi far gone in love for *Sedgewycke?*"

"What have we been talking about if not Aaron. A fine young man of good family and far more wealthy than any have guessed." Everhart grimaced slightly. "He'd have made Georgi an excellent husband."

"Which plan you'd approve?" asked Vincent, seeing more of Everhart's dislike of the notion than Everhart knew he felt.

"Well, I'm not sure . . ."

"Academic in any case," interrupted Vincent. He added in an offhand manner: "Aaron is for Cassie."

"So he is." Everhart grinned, a quick flash of teeth and a lightening of the tension around his eyes. "So he is . . ." He sobered. "Not that that helps Georgi, of course."

"But consolation for Georgi is not so far away as one might think," suggested Vincent. He noted the strange look Everhart tossed his way, but ignored it since he was already thinking up plots whereby he might promote Georgi's very obvious desire to wring a declaration from Everhart. Such a plot must be very carefully designed if Georgi were not to say it went against her sense of honor to carry it through.

"I would never have guessed you only twenty-three," said Everhart. "You have far more maturity and self-confidence than most men of that age."

"Most men were not such fools as to run off to the wars at not yet fifteen. I was always a well-grown brat. Grandfather, bless him, did not give up hope of finding me and I can admit now I was never more pleased than when he did. He was more than a little shocked to discover me . . . educated, shall we say . . . beyond my years. Then he did me no service bringing me to the

Place and overseeing my education for the next year or two before sending me off to Oxford where I fell in with all the worst sort of choice spirits—bored, of course, by the more serious or the far greener lad I *should* have chosen for friend."

"I see. Except, given the scenario you draw, I should have heard gossip of your excesses and I have not."

"No. Among other things which I learned in the army, was that one always covered one's arse so that no blame could fall on one's unwary head." Vincent chuckled. "There is also the fact that far too much of what is considered entertainment by the wilder element with which I'm associated bores me. I've no desire to tip the Charlies the double or chase the comets through the slums in St. Giles, so I do not participate. I box and spend more time than anyone else I know with a certain expert in the Italian theory of swordplay. I enjoy racing and other such sports. If I drink too much, and gamble to the edge of ruin and have in keeping one highflier after another, why what else is there to do?"

"I cannot recall ever meeting your father . . ."

"My parents and Georgi's died in a boating accident. Georgi has spent her life since she was six here at the Place. I spent my school vacations here until, at fourteen, I ran away."

"Why did Lord Tivington not buy you your colors once you were of an age to have them?"

Vincent shrugged, his eyes looking at something only he could see. "Have you ever been in battle, my lord?"

"No, I've no desire for that experience. War is a nightmare I hope I'll never be made to endure."

"Nightmare. You understand, do you not? I had nightmares for years. I was with Abercromby's ill-fated Dutch invasion. Disillusionment about such things as honor and glory came early. After my last battle I was discovered," said Vincent, the characteristic dryness of his speech very much in evidence, "pinned beneath a dead horse, an officer bleeding to death in my arms. It was not that I was a green lad who had never seen blood spilled, but the officer was married and his last minutes were spent giving me civil messages for his wife and children. There was a macabre drawing room air to it—polite requests on his part, polite promises on mine—which, for a time, turned my brain, I think. Around us was such chaos: hand-to-hand fighting, the thunder of exploding artillery, the surge of men and horses as the battle went over the top of us twice . . ." Vincent upended his tankard and called for another round of beer. "I suppose it's no wonder I sent a message to Grandfather asking him to get me home. I've often wondered if I'd still be in uniform, or, more likely, dead, except for that experience."

Everhart let a moment pass in silence and watched as Vincent pulled himself together. "Did you deliver the messages?"

"Yes. Mrs. Clark received me and Grandfather, listened to what I had to say, and excused herself. Her daughters were brought in by a weak-chinned governessy person. I said my piece, they curtsied and were led out again. I am certain two of them would not have recognized their father if he had walked in the door. The eldest didn't seem particularly interested in my words, but gave me a saucy smile, and a speculative look. I had been introduced to the muslin company—mostly the drabs who travel in the tail of an army—early in my enlistment. I made a bet with myself that that young lady would, unless married young, join them." Vincent glanced up, met Everhart's eyes, his own twinkling wickedly. "She is now Mrs. Spence. If you listen to gossip at all, which you suggested you do, then you will have heard of Mrs. Spence. I am quite puffed up in my own esteem to think that I was so perspicacious at such an early age!"

Everhart hid a grin. "Mrs. Spence is entirely a respectable married lady."

"*Of course* she is," agreed Vincent blandly.

Everhart gave him a look. Vincent chuckled. After a moment his lordship asked, "Why has Georgi not been presented? She must be the same age as your other cousin who has been out for three years now."

"Grandfather's decision, of course. Year after year my unmarried aunts are loud in favor of her presentation. This last year I think she'd have been all right, but up to then, Georgi agreed she was not ready for one."

"She will come out this coming spring?"

"She very likely will—poor dear."

"She has charm, looks, and, I presume, a good dower. She will very likely be the rage so why do you call her poor dear?"

"Georgi, all the rage? No, not Georgi. Not that she couldn't if she willed it, but she will study it all, come to the conclusion it is shallow and unlikely to offer amusement for more than three weeks at the outside and, very likely, demand to be brought home very soon after her presentation at the Queen's Drawing Room."

"Every young girl dreams . . ."

"Georgi?" Vincent interrupted scornfully. "Where will she find a game of chess? Or time for the books she will, with great enthusiasm, take home from Hookham's? She will resent time wasted in fittings. She will discover the young women with whom she is required to talk both insipid and ignorant. She will hate the hypocrisy. She will disapprove of the gambling and drinking—*especially* the gambling, given the poverty she'll see which might be alleviated if that money were spent in more charitable ways. Oh, there are a hundred things she will dislike for every advantage she finds. She will enjoy the theater and opera and, given Georgi's love of music, perhaps she will enjoy the musical evenings and, heaven forfend that I be made to escort her there, a performance of the Society For the Preservation of Ancient Music! There will be bookstores and libraries where she may browse. Due to Grandfather's interests, there will be invitations to the smaller political gatherings where she may enjoy serious conversation and where she will shine . . . I am boring on forever, am I not? Georgi and Grandfather are my two favorite people and Georgi comes first by quite a bit even there. I will have to spend more time than I like among people I detest to protect my brat from the dangers she'll face as a green girl just introduced to the *ton*. If she were married, however, I could leave that duty to her husband . . . assuming he were a right one who could be trusted to guide her steps until she found her footing."

"Why don't you marry her yourself."

"Myself? Marry Georgi? That would have the ugly smack of incest, my lord. She may be my cousin rather than my sister, but our relationship is far more the latter than the former."

Everhart relaxed. "I'll share your responsibilities, if you like. When she comes to London, I mean. That way you need not spend quite so much time doing the pretty, which is, I believe, a role you don't care to play. I, on the other hand, enjoy much of the Season—although not the squeezes where one cannot find one's friends or, if one is so lucky as to do so, one cannot find a quiet corner in which to converse with them."

Vincent nursed the last of his brew. "I will take you up on that offer, Everhart, assuming you do not care if your name becomes associated with hers. You could find yourself leg-shackled to her before the Season is over if you do not take care," he added slyly, watching his guest's features closely.

Everhart paused in the process of raising his mug for one long last drink. He lowered his arm before taking it. "Married to Georgi? But she is . . . no, I forget. She is *not* too young." He laughed, an embarrassed sound to it. "I would not find it a hardship to take young Georgi to wife, I think, but not—" He frowned. "—so long as she is suffering that infatuation for Sedgewycke."

Vincent shook his head. It was, he decided, very difficult to get a notion out of his lordship's mind once the notion had taken up lodging there. Should he tell Everhart that Sedgie was another of Georgi's adopted brothers and that she'd no more marry Aaron than she would himself? Or should he leave Everhart in doubt, on the theory that what one has to work to achieve one appreciates the more? Vincent, finding his mug empty, decided he must work off his overindulgence of Goodwife Potter's cookery. "I planned to ride over the Place's acres this afternoon, my lord. Perhaps we will meet again soon."

"I hope we will. You have not come in my way in the past, Vincent, so I have not gotten to know you. I hope you will not be such a stranger to me in future." He held out his hand, and Vincent grasped it firmly. The two men soon parted company very much in charity with each other, although Everhart might have been a trifle wary if he'd known with what complacence Vincent contemplated the circumstances of their future meetings and how much they had to do with his well-loved cousin's future!

Ten

Nanny was as difficult to say good-bye to as usual, not that Georgi tried too hard, but it meant she was, as expected, late returning home. She'd hoped that sneaking in by way of the back entrance and up the servants' staircase would answer. It didn't: Her Aunt Anne sat by her window, her mending in her lap. "Aunt? You wished to speak with me?"

"I am rather displeased with you, Georgi."

"How have I erred, Aunt?" It never did to contradict her Aunt Anne. That only made the woman more stubborn.

"We have, I believe, taught you certain responsibilities toward guests, child. You are failing in your duties as hostess."

"How have I failed?"

"In several ways. Elliot has complained often you are nowhere to be found when he has wished a game of billiards or to go riding."

Georgi's lips compressed tightly. It would not do to explain to her aunt exactly why she failed in *that* putative duty.

"Then there is your Aunt Melicent. She feels you give her far less attention than your relationship deserves."

"She has never wished my attendance in the past, Aunt. I did not know she had changed."

"It did not occur to you to ask?"

"No. I do not look upon our kin as guests in my grandfather's house, but as family who will treat the Place as if it were their home. I cannot see how they would wish to be treated like strangers."

"But there *is* a stranger, is there not?"

"Mrs. Compton? No one can accuse me of slighting Mrs. Compton, Aunt. I say everything which is proper to her and I have enjoyed her company often. Why are you really scolding me, Aunt?"

Aunt Anne sighed. It was always so with Georgi. She *would* rush straight to a point. "My dear, it cannot have escaped your notice that your Aunt Melicent has high hopes of a match between Lord Everhart and your cousin. She fears your behavior may have driven a wedge between the couple when, as she tells me is so, all was going on quite prosperously during the Season."

"What I have noticed is that my aunt throws Cassie at his lordship's head as often as possible and in the most vulgar of fashions."

"Georgi! You are insulting. Melicent is too much the lady to do anything of the sort! You will apologize for even *thinking* she might do something so ill-bred."

Georgi wondered if her aunt believed what she said. It seemed she did. "I will apologize for *saying* it, Aunt, but I will not apologize for my thoughts. Lord Everhart has no interest in Cassie, by the way."

"You are privy to his lordship's thoughts?" asked her aunt coldly.

"In this respect I am. His lordship believes me no more than a schoolroom brat. That first evening he came to dinner and saw that my aunt and Cassie were here, he thought to use me as a buffer and asked me to save him from them. He has no wish to wed Cassie and is determined to avoid any traps set for him." Having said her piece, Georgi waited for a scold or derogatory comments about coxcombs who would say such things to a young girl. Instead her aunt asked:

"How can he think you such a child?"

Georgi debated lying, then shrugged the thought away. Lying never answered. "Grandfather and I did not tell you how we first met his lordship." She described the scene in the churchyard. "I know you will scold me for such hoydenish behavior, but you will admit that it has served to deceive Lord Everhart, and I cannot be thought to rival my cousin. I say again, however, that Lord Everhart feels he is hunted by Aunt Mclicent and wishes she would accept he has no interest in Cassie. His story of their London experience is quite different from what Aunt Melicent must have told you, by the way."

"Then someone prevaricates. You will insist it is Melicent and not his lordship, but you can have no knowledge of the deviousness of men. Men are much more likely to tell fables than are women, my child."

Again Georgi wondered if her aunt believed what she said and again was forced to conclude she did. "Aunt, has it occurred to you that *Cassie's* wishes might be of some import?"

"She is a child. Young girls must be led."

"But led into a marriage actively disliked?"

"That would be wrong. You cannot tell me, however, there would be anything to dislike about becoming Everhart's countess!"

Georgi debated arguing that but decided it wouldn't do. Aunt Anne was far too conventional to be convinced that a mere Mister one loved was a better fate than a social coup that raised one's status. "Aunt, I have discussed this with Grandfather. He has other notions for Cassie," said Georgi desperately.

"Father has plans?"

"Yes."

Her assertion was met by a brief silence.

"Why has he not explained them to the family, then?"

"I believe he wishes to see them to completion first."

"How can he weave alternate plots when the only eligible gentleman available is Lord Everhart?"

"Perhaps he feels she is too young to wed immediately."

"Georgi, *you* are too young to know of the difficulties my brother and Melicent face just now, but Cassie
is *not* too young to help."

"If," said Georgi, completely exasperated, and therefore losing all sense of caution, "you mean Elliot's
losses at table and turf, why should Cassie be sacrificed
to bring them around? *Elliot* should be the one to suffer."

"How have you learned of Elliot's peccadilloes?" It
was a rhetorical question. Anne well knew the answer.
"It is outrageous what my father will discuss with you!
He has no business explaining such things to a chit not
yet out who, even then, should have no awareness of the
seamier side of life. I will have words with him, Georgi.
He must be brought to his senses and cease treating you
as if you were a boy and his heir, which you are not and
cannot be. As for you, you are in need of discipline for
the impertinence of arguing with me. You will remain in
this room until I decide differently."

Anne rose to her feet and, in a stately manner, exited,
shutting the door quietly behind her. Georgi grimaced
and wondered who might brave her aunt's anger to bring
her the book she was currently reading. It was MacGill's
Travels in Turkey, Italy and Russia and, if she remembered rightly, it lay on the right-hand side of her desk.

She moved to her window and looked out. The old

oak had often been her friend during past incarcerations. She'd avoided just punishment by climbing out onto a limb and down to the ground, but that was no longer possible. Aunt Marie had witnessed one of Georgi's unauthorized exits and the next day Lord Tivington's head gardener and the man who oversaw the woodlands gracing the property arrived with ladders and saws and several feet were cut from any limb which came near to touching the house.

Later Georgi learned by careful probing that her aunt disliked the sound of branches tapping the walls. In any case, the old line of escape was gone. Georgi knelt by her window, her arms laying on the sill and her chin on one wrist. She stared out into the summer dusk at nothing in particular.

She was still there when several acorns rattled against the window. The noise startled her and she jerked her head, banging it painfully against the frame. Another acorn hit the window and she searched the tree for her visitor, grinning when Vincent pushed aside a branch and she could see his face. He grimaced at her, and chuckling, she opened the window.

"Well, brat? I hear you forgot yourself again," he whispered.

"So I did. I'll never learn."

"Very likely not," he agreed. "Aunt Anne is steaming. There was a row in the library between she and Grandfather, but it's not spread elsewhere. Yet."

"You want to know what happened?"

"Brat, how can I decide which way to jump when I've no notion what mischief you've been up to this time?"

In a singsong voice Georgi reported the conversation between herself and her Aunt Anne. It was, very nearly, a verbatim report, Georgi having that useful thing, an excellent memory. "So you see, I really put my foot in it," she finished. "Grandfather will not be pleased I've given his head for washing. He does not *like* how the aunts go about washing one's head."

"Nobody with any sense likes it. I'll take Aunt aside and confirm your information concerning Lord Everhart's intentions. Or, rather, his lack of them! That will do much to undermine her fit of pique. Beyond that I don't know what to do. How long did she keep you incarcerated the last time you set up her back?"

"Nearly a week."

"We can't have *that*. I couldn't bear it here without your leavening influence! Not with our dear cousins' in residence. I'll see to it, Georgi. Trust me."

"Normally I wouldn't mind the isolation. Having an unexceptional excuse for avoiding Elliot suits me to a cow's thumb, but I'll admit I'll rue missing your visit. At least I presume it will be as usual, and you will be off in a very few days!"

"Perhaps not this time. I fear you will have to put up with Elliot, because I fully intend having you free so that I may not be bored to tears. Grandfather," he ended with a grin, "will only put up with me so long and that is not long enough to fill my days. Take heart. 'Bye brat." He disappeared.

"Vincent!"

She heard a muffled curse before his head reappeared. "This better be important, brat. I just tore a bloody great hole in my trousers."

"Oh dear. I'll mend them for you, when I'm free."

"That you will not. I know how you love your needle and I don't wish great awkward stitches marching across my rear. Now what is the problem?"

"Would you ask Grandfather to bring me my book? Only he can do so with impunity. And perhaps he might indulge me to that extent even if he will not interfere with my aunt's discipline, especially if he is angry at me himself for leaving him open to her ranting." She told Vincent where the volume was to be found.

"I'll ask him. Now I am off, so if there is ought else be quick about it."

"Nothing. Thank you for coming, Vincent."

"Really, brat, did you think I'll leave you to suffer without a thought to your comfort? I might not have loaned Elliot my blunt when he needed it, but I'll sell off my team and even my best sword, the Italian one with that ridiculous huge emerald in the hilt, if *you* need it. Now, this time it is good-bye." His voice was muffled and she had to listen hard to hear the rest: "Don't despair. You'll be downstairs again before you know it."

Georgi let him go, knowing he would lose patience if she persisted in detaining him. Climbing trees for secret consultations with his brat of a cousin wasn't behavior commensurate with his dignity. Georgi giggled as she thought of his being caught with torn breeches. He'd never live it down. Then time dragged for her. It was long after dinner when a light tap indicated someone at her door. Georgi opened it and found her grandfather there. He held out a stack of books to her. "Thank you."

He didn't answer but she didn't expect it. It was a rule of such discipline that she be considered in Coventry and no one was to speak to her. Grandfather, even when he disagreed, had always left the decision to her aunts concerning the need for such discipline. Having handed over the books, he turned and walked away. Sadly, Georgi watched him go. She felt no particular guilt for having argued with her aunt. She felt a great deal for having brought that same aunt's wrath down on his gray head!

True to his word, Vincent discovered a moment after dinner when Aunt Anne was alone. He approached her and taking her arm, invited her to walk in the garden with him. Given he was already helping her to her feet, she had either to go or to make a scene. There was something in the stern features of her nephew which made her accede to his wishes.

"You will have to apologize to my grandfather, Aunt," he said, sternly, once they were along on the paths through the knot garden.

"Apologize to . . . ?"

"Yes," he interrupted before she could finish. It never did to allow Aunt Anne an inch in an argument, but to rush her right through it. "You were quite in the wrong. I had lunch with Everhart today. He feels harassed to the point he'd leave the area if he could, but the estate is still in such a muddle he cannot. My Aunt Melicent is well known to be on the catch for a rich husband for Cassie. She was thought to have a Mr. Davenant in her eye until she thought up the plan to draw Everhart into her trap."

Anne paced several steps before she said, grudgingly, "Since you feel you must report it, I will listen to what Everhart has told you. Already I feel it must be a lie. Melicent is too much the lady to stoop to anything smelling of a trick."

"You should not judge others by your own values, Aunt. Aunt Melicent would stoop to anything. In this particular case she took part in a conversation she intended Lord Everhart to overhear. In it she deliberately smeared Cassie's reputation, telling her bosom beau, who was in the plot, she despaired of her daughter's behavior, which was growing decidedly fast, and feared the chit would lose her reputation before she got her married off."

"Everhart told you this?"

"Yes. It is the exact same trick which trapped Stravager . . ."

"The Viscount Littledean?" interrupted Anne.

"Yes. Littledean told me the story after he and his new wife decided to lead separate lives. He had much the same reputation with the ladies that Everhart enjoys, which isn't *bad* but has *a touch* of the rake about it. When Everhart overheard the chit was ripe for a spree, why should he not try his hand? Stravager was caught seducing his innocent. Everhart was a trifle more knowing and escaped without compromising Cassie. But Aunt Melicent is not to be thwarted. She followed him here. Now the story becomes farce. Everhart fell into the not unnatural mistake that our Georgi was barely out of the schoolroom—if that. Seeing he'd been followed by Melicent, he enlisted Georgi to give him protection whenever there was a possibility he might find himself alone with Cassie. Georgi has done so, but not entirely for Everhart's sake. I have it on good authority Cassie has given her silly heart elsewhere. The match is not so unexceptional as one with Everhart, but a far cry from one with Davenant who is a rank outsider. Believe me! Only that man's wealth keeps him on the edges of the *ton!* No," he added, when his aunt would have asked the next obvious question, "I will not tell you more. Grandfather knows the whole and approves. That should suffice."

"Then why did my father not tell me so?"

"He is a man of honor. He cannot tell you what he has promised not to tell."

"Why such secrecy?"

"Aunt Melicent."

"Oh." Anne's lips compressed. "You mean she would attempt to put an iron in the spokes."

"She would. I don't believe I know a more stubborn wrong-headed woman. Once she takes a notion there is no changing her mind. She has said Lord Everhart will wed Cassie and she will not be thwarted."

"You are suggesting I should keep this from her."

"I think you must," said Vincent gently.

"I wish you had not told me."

"I'll be honest, Aunt, and tell you I would not have, except I cannot have my brat tucked away in Coventry when I wish her to play with me."

Anne chuckled. "You are a rogue, Vincent, and I can never resist your wiles. But," she sighed, "I should have listened to Georgi's words which I did not. I fear I, too, can be a trifle stubborn."

So you can, dear Aunt, thought Vincent. *So you can.*

She added, "I am sure Georgi deserves punishment for any number of things I know nothing of, so some time in her room will not harm her. However that may be, I will allow her to come down to dinner tomorrow evening."

"Breakfast? She's innocent of all charges, you know."

Anne sighed. "Luncheon, then."

"I see. Having said she must be punished, you cannot admit you erred. She must be punished to some extent."

"Vincent, do not push your luck. I have agreed to luncheon, but I firmly believe there have been machinations for which she deserves much more if I only knew of them."

Vincent thought of finding his Georgi alone with Everhart along the river and decided that, honorably, he could not push to better things for her. "Then I've done what I can and shall, as you suggest, leave well enough alone. May I tell her she may come down tomorrow?"

"No you may not. And don't attempt to cut any more wheedles, m'lad!"

Aunt and nephew grinned at each other and Vincent asked about the pineapples she had recently added to her extensive succession houses. They got on quite prosperously after that and were still discussing such things when Elliot came up to them and, interrupting, suggested a game of billiards.

"Won't Mrs. Compton play with you?"

"Can she play?"

"If she can't, perhaps you could teach her." Vincent could see the wheels turning in his cousin's head, could see him imagining his arms around the widow while he showed her how to hold the cue, how to slide it through one's fingers. . . . "I believe you will find her writing letters in the small salon," added Vincent.

"Do you think," asked his aunt when Elliot trotted away, "that he should be encouraged to spend so much time in our guest's company? He is, according to Melicent, overly susceptible to feminine wiles and forever in the muslin company. I should hate to find that he has insulted a guest in our house by stepping over the line of what is gentlemanly behavior."

"Mrs. Compton is quite able to take care of herself, Aunt." Vincent hid a grin, knowing the plot laid to trap Elliot. He must remember to tell Georgi how he had forwarded their machinations. *She'll be quite pleased with me,* he decided.

She was. He told her as they rode cross-country to the village and she was laughing when they met Lord Everhart and Sedgewycke. "You!" she said to the latter. "You are supposed to be visiting my uncle. Why are you here?"

"I'm there and back and have her father's permission to court my Cassie!" He grinned happily. "I know your grandfather hasn't said I may return, but *you* are trespassing or you'd not have known of my existence."

"We'll keep it a secret. Oh, do you remember my cousin, Vincent?"

"Of course." Small talk held them for some minutes but they soon sorted themselves out and went on as a foursome.

"How did it go with my uncle?" asked Georgi, sliding her mare between Everhart and Sedgewycke's geldings.

"We've reached a tentative agreement as to settlements and he agreed to say nothing to his wife until I've had my chance with Cassie. He's not so sanguine as Lady Melicent is about Everhart coming up to scratch, and prefers a bird in hand. He's not completely happy. He hoped Cassie's marriage would cover his son's losses, but I told him I didn't see why I should pay that piper for him and he's a fair enough man when away from his wife! He agreed."

"I don't see why you should, either, and all will be well in any case, assuming," she said blithely without thought to whom she spoke, "we manage to wed Elliot to the Golden Widow."

"The widow?" asked Sedgewycke just as Vincent muttered, "Georgi, Georgi!"

"Blast," said Georgi inelegantly. "I should not have said that. You will forget it immediately."

Everhart turned a speculative look on Georgi. He, too, gave no thought to tact: "Do you think Elliot's mother would approve a tie between her son and the vulgar widow?" A sound from Sedgewycke snapped his look toward the younger man and he remembered the widow was Aaron's sister. "Forgive me," he said. "I should not have said that."

"But it is true," said Sedgewycke sadly. "She is vulgar. She had, from an early age, an aching need for money which no one in the family understood. She would beg coins from total strangers! It was embarrassing. Her meeting with Compton was fortuitous, actually. He may have been a cit, but he was a gentle man if not a gentleman. I admired him," finished Sedgie, defiantly.

Georgi squeezed his arm. "From what you say and what Alicia told me, he sounds a man deserving of liking and respect. Don't get on your high horse."

Sedgewycke bit his lip. "Georgi, from what you let slip, I assume you have a plan to marry your cousin to my sister."

"Yes."

"You'll not say more?"

"No."

"I must say more: I do not approve."

"Discuss it with your sister. She knows all and has decided Elliot will do as a vehicle for returning her to her place in the *ton.*" Again Georgi squeezed Sedgie's arm. "Grandfather will give her his countenance, you know. He will not let her flounder or fail in her wishes."

"Elliot is not a man to whom I'd wish any woman married."

"Discuss that with her as well, will you not?" When he didn't answer, she added, "I have."

Everhart, listening to her, wondered how he'd originally mistaken her for a fifteen-year-old. All he had to do was close his eyes and he *heard* her maturity, a maturity which she all too often allowed to slip by the wayside when indulging in some hoydenish trick! Another thought occurred to him, and Everhart realized that he was innocent of one thing. Those times he'd thought himself perverted for having sudden urges to make love to a mere child were explained satisfactorily. His mind might have believed her a schoolroom miss, but he'd obviously known otherwise at a deeper level.

Had Vincent truly suggested he marry her? Lord Everhart's blood flew faster through his veins and an unwanted warmth elsewhere made riding distinctly uncomfortable. Marry her? He forced himself to control his urges and shook his head. In most ways, despite her age, she was very young. He would be taking advantage of her green emotions if he were to woo her now before she'd had so much as a few weeks of a Season. He wondered if he could talk Lord Tivington into bringing her out this coming Little Season so that he wouldn't have to wait so very long to put his fate to the touch.

Everhart blinked, jerking his reins in a way he'd have considered quite unforgivably ham-handed if he'd noticed. His horse reacted as any well-trained animal would to such inconsiderate and confusing signals. His lordship soothed the animal even as he accepted the fact that he had suddenly and irrevocably decided he would marry Georgi as soon as, with honor, he possibly could!

"Something bothering you?" asked Vincent, who dropped back with him as he slowed more and more, allowing Sedgewycke and Georgi to ride on ahead.

"Bothering me?" Everhart's eyes narrowed with humor, and he grinned widely. "Bothering me? It *was,* but it no longer is. I wonder if Lord Tivington will be free this afternoon?" He turned a speculative eye on Vincent and quirked his head.

"If you mean to take my advice and marry the chit, may I suggest I bring him to a meeting somewhere outside the Place? If you come to formally ask for Georgi's hand, it will be all over the house before you ever come out of his study. I can imagine the uproar *that* would cause! I do not like uproars. I have not cared for them since my army days. Perhaps we could meet at the mill to discuss it and the bridge as my grandfather told me you and he should do. It will be quite unexceptional for you to meet that way and your business may be done with no one the wiser."

Everhart hedged. "We go too fast. I have not approached Georgi. I do not know if I am at all agreeable to her and fear that, given she has so little experience, she cannot possibly *know* what suits her. She might say yes and find all too soon she has erred."

"The only incompatibility I see between you is that you spend more time in London than she will like until she develops friendships of the sort she'll enjoy. The problem will be to keep her there long enough she discovers the whole of the *ton* is not pleasure-seeking and without a thought in their collective heads but of the latest fashions and the most titillating of crim-cons . . ."

"My mother will help me find her agreeable friends."

"Ah. I had forgotten your mother. I attended one or two of her salons with Tom Moore a year or so ago. She still holds them?"

"She does. And she will welcome a daughter-in-law who enters into her interests which, I believe from some talk concerning books we've had, that Georgi will."

"Oh, yes, definitely she will." Vincent was one of three people who knew of Georgi's novel writing. "I would mention your mother when you talk to Grandfather. He has been out of society for a time and might not know of her interest in the world of art and literature."

"This still does not solve the problem that she is nothing but a green girl despite her advanced years! She will be courted and petted and become the rage and I will lose her to some encroaching half-pay officer with more than his fair share of charm!"

"You go from avuncular uncle to possessive lover in the blink of the eye! You will not change back just as quickly?"

"I will not. You cannot know how difficult the pose of uncle was at times. She is a delight."

On those words they noticed that the two in front had pulled up. "You have been telling secrets, Vincent!" said Georgi. "I can always tell when you wish to keep something from me. Now don't spoil a perfectly good day by being stubborn, old friend. You know I can always make you tell me."

"How long has it been since you last tried, brat?"

Georgi tipped her head and laughed. "Three or four years, I think."

"Since then I've quite grown up. Besides, those were secrets I *wished* pried from me. You never learn anything I've no desire to tell you."

"I don't?" She pouted for a moment, before grinning again. "Now that puts me in my place does it not? Shall we race?"

"To what point?"

"Over the bridge, ending on the other side. Whoever crosses first wins." She pointed toward the distant willows lining the river above the mill, the roof of which could be seen where they thinned near the mill race.

"Wins what?"

"Who cares?" she said with a laugh. "Shall we?"

Her mare danced in response to the excitement she felt in her rider. Georgi easily controlled her, her excited features enthusing the men. She lined them up and shouted, "Ready! *Go!*"

Pounding hooves threw up clods of dry summer earth. Everhart soon pulled slightly ahead of Vincent. Sedgewycke rode nose-to-nose with Georgi's mare, the two losing ground as they neared the river. Georgi was not surprised when Vincent and Everhart pulled up on the other side in a tie, walking their horses in a large circle to cool them as they waited for Georgi and Sedgewycke.

Sedgewycke suddenly put on an effort. His gelding

stretched and sped up. He was a few yards ahead of her and crossing the bridge as she reached it. The men were suddenly yelling something and waving their arms but she could not distinguish the words and pounded onto the bridge, which swayed dangerously, and with a loud crack of timbers, it tilted. Her mare scrabbled for footing and very nearly made it when Georgi lost her seat. She felt herself fall. . . .

Georgi faded in and out of consciousness, but not to the extent she didn't know she was in Everhart's arms which was, she thought, very nice, or would be if only her head didn't ache so badly. The arms holding her close were comforting, and so too the words she was very likely imagining.

"I've lost you. I can't lose you, Georgi. I won't lose you. You're mine, Georgi, and I'll be damned if I'll give you time to look about you. Somehow I'll teach you to love me as I love you. Georgi, look at me. Georgi, Georgi . . ."

She moaned, the headache worsening.

"Georgi? Georgi, speak to me . . ."

Perhaps she hadn't imagined it? "What can I say," she muttered. "What can I say? You saved my life . . ."

Another fear clutched at Everhart: Would she marry him out of gratitude? He didn't want *that*. "That was nothing. Besides, it was all three of us." He pulled her around so he could see her face, his hands holding her steady. "Look at me, Georgi. You heard what I said. I know you did. I don't want you to answer me now because right now we are too emotional and you might say yes for all the wrong reasons . . . Georgi? Why do you look at me like that?"

Surely she must have imagined it. "I don't know what you are saying. I heard you ask me to speak to you . . ."

Everhart sighed. She looked so bewildered. And it

truly was not the time to propose to a woman when she
had a bad bump on her head, was soaked through, and
had been close to drowning. "Never mind, my love. We
will have a more appropriate time and I will tell you all
over again."

"What did you call me?" Georgi almost forgot she
was soaking wet, the water dripping from her habit in
runnels. She forgot she was cold, that she had nearly lost
her life. *"What* did you say?"

Everhart flushed. "A slip of the tongue. Shouldn't
have said it. You'd best forget it."

"Forget it?" She smiled. "Then you can forget that
I'm thanking you for my life . . ." She thrust forward,
forgetting her sore head. Her arms encircled his neck
and her lips found his in an enthusiastic, if awkward,
kiss.

A swift turn of his eyes showed Everhart that the
other two were preoccupied with saving the mare. For
an unforgettable moment, Everhart took control, sa-
vored the passion he recognized in her untutored
response, and then, reluctantly, unwound her arms and
pushed her away. They stared at each other. It was
Georgi's turn to blush.

"I'll forget it until the next time," he said softly.
"Now, my girl, you behave or you'll have us both in a
peck of trouble. We must get you dry and warm and see
your bump hasn't resulted in a concussion. The Manor
is closest, I believe. Sedgewycke," he called, noting the
mare, limping, was finally on dry land, "bring up my
mount, if you would. I'll carry Georgi to the Manor
where she may get out of these wet things. Vincent, I
think you'd best go to the Place and get clothes and perhaps her aunt and bring them to the Manor. Anyone
object?"

Since, by this time, Georgi could no longer repress

shudders induced by the wet material which was chilled by a stiff breeze, no one argued. Vincent took off his jacket and wrapped her in it before lifting her into the saddle before Everhart. "I'll bring Aunt Marie, Georgi. Behave yourself, now."

Georgi's teeth chattered. Everhart's arms were comforting, warming. She wished she need never leave their protection. It was nice to lean against his chest. Wool had such an odd smell when wet, she thought, and relaxed another notch. She felt his arms tighten around her. But her head throbbed and reaction hit. She might have died! Georgi trembled all over.

"It's all right now, my child. We're safe. *We are safe.*" Everhart, more worried than he allowed himself to reveal, repeated the words whenever she began to shake and mutter. His voice seemed to soothe her. But what was wrong with her? Could she have come down with a fever so quickly? The words she muttered were irrational, those of someone in a delirium. He felt her forehead and found she did indeed have a fever. Everhart urged his horse to greater effort, and upon arriving at the front door to the Manor, yelled for a groom to go for the doctor. At once!

Sedgewycke, coming along behind, canceled the order as Everhart stalked into the house, carrying his beloved burden. "Take the gig," he said, "and get Nanny Worrick. Tell her Georgi was in the river, has a vicious bump on the head, might have died, and is *very suddenly* sick. We'll do what we can to warm her, but I don't know what else to do. Yes I do. Send someone else to the Place. Tell them the situation is urgent. And *hurry.*"

Sedgewycke, too, ran lightly inside. He found Hamish giving orders in a staccato voice before hurrying up the stairs. Aaron followed, entering the main bedroom in the valet's wake. He bit his lip. Everhart had

Georgi half out of her habit and was struggling with her limp figure to remove her skirt, which huge and wet, persisted in sticking to her limbs.

"Help me, blast it. She's freezing." Hamish went to his assistance at once.

Sedgewycke hesitated. "We'll compromise her . . ."

"Better that than *dead*. She has a raging fever."

"Three men . . . She'll never recover from her embarrassment." But Sedgewycke joined the other two and they soon had Georgi in one of Everhart's nightshirts and wrapped in several blankets.

"Now she's freezing again. Damn and blast, why didn't I immediately bring her here? Why did I wait to see if the two of you got that damned mare up and out of the water?" Everhart held the bundle which was Georgi close, rocking her back and forth. "Georgi, Georgi, love. Oh, Georgi, my love . . ."

A bath and hot water arrived. Georgi was carefully unwrapped and, nightshirt and all, dunked. She was still in the tub when Nanny stomped up the stairs, trailed by two maids from the village who had been hired by Hamish to help in the house.

Nanny took one look at the three worried men hovering over her old charge and straightened to her full four foot seven inches. She pointed at the door. "Out. Now." The men went. At once Nanny turned on the maids. "You did not see three men in here with my girl dressed that way."

She glowered. The girls looked one to the other and shook their heads. Nanny had the reputation of being something of a witch. The girls, fearing her, would not open their mouths. Nanny was satisfied by their assurances. When someone from the Place arrived, it would be assumed Nanny and the girls had undressed her last baby.

"Let me see now . . ." She checked the water temperature, and Georgi's condition, which wasn't good.

Nanny bit her lip. "Let's get her to bed." The sturdy village lasses were quite capable of lifting such a little thing as Georgi. They did so and between them were putting her into a clean nightshirt when Georgi's aunts arrived along with the abigail Lord Tivington had hired for his granddaughter while in London.

Georgi muttered constantly but nothing which was intelligible. She was watched just as constantly, Nanny and her aunts, Marie and Anne, dividing the nursing among themselves with the help of her dresser, June Darwin, and the village girls. Sedgewycke was congratulated for not sending for the doctor, but not until after he'd had something of a turn-up with Everhart who had forgotten the doctor was old-fashioned and rarely called anywhere by anyone. For three days Everhart's bedroom was a sickroom into which he was not allowed. For three days he paced the hall except when someone forced him to sit to table, where he played with his food and drank far more than he ate, or when Hamish drugged him lightly and led him to a bed for much-needed sleep. On the fourth day Lord Tivington joined Everhart in his perambulation up and down the wide hall. They made their third turn before Everhart realized he had company. "Lord Tivington . . ."

"My lord Everhart. You'll have a new problem on your hands by the time my Georgi is well."

The dry humor in the old man's voice caught Everhart's attention. "I will?"

"Hmm. Buying a replacement for the carpet on which we're treading."

Everhart laughed. It was weak but it was a laugh and Hamish, hidden behind the narrowly open door of the room Everhart was using while Georgi used his, drew in and let go a deep breath of relief.

"I care naught for the carpet, which wasn't in the best of condition to begin with. I care a great deal that I allowed Georgi to come to grief. I should have known . . . should have refused . . . should have fixed that bridge long ago but . . ."

"But," interrupted Lord Tivington, "you have had much on your plate and everyone with any sense uses the ford. The accident was an accident. Or, if we must apportion blame, I am at fault. I should have had the thing pulled down years ago. But I do not believe we have any guilt in this. Accidents happen. This one happened to Georgi."

"She is so sick. I do not understand it."

"If Georgi has a weakness, it is that a damp chill can send her into fever quick as winking. You could not know that. The day was warm enough, so Vincent, who might have guessed, didn't think there'd be a problem. But you had been riding hard and were overheated from exercise; cold water and a breeze did the damage."

"She has suffered this way in the past?"

"Once or twice. You mustn't worry so. Nanny always pulls her through. She will again."

"Perhaps someone should learn Nanny's little ways," said Everhart with some heat. "Nanny will not live forever and might not be available if this were to happen again."

"Calm yourself. The procedure for her cure is well known. Her aunts learned years ago. At the moment her new maid is helping with her care and will learn what to do. Rarely is it necessary, of course." Tivington studied his host with a twinkle in his own eye. "You have an interest in Georgi's cure beyond the guilt you mentioned?"

"Yes." The word exploded from Everhart. "Yes and yes and yes." He took several quick strides away from where Lord Tivington leaned on his cane and came back in a more moderate fashion. "I apologize for my outburst," he said a trifle pompously. "This is not how I'd have wished to approach you, but I must. I wish to marry your granddaughter, Lord Tivington. Have I permission to woo her and, I hope with all my heart, win her hand in marriage?"

Lord Tivington quirked his brow. His lips twitched once and then he stared sardonically at Everhart's rather pompous stance—obviously assumed as a defense against revealing more of his emotions.

"Which granddaughter?" asked his lordship, unable to repress a reprehensible sense of the ridiculous.

Eleven

Everhart's face was a picture of bewilderment. "Which . . . ?"

"I repeat, which of my granddaughters will you have?"

Everhart blinked. Having lost interest in anything around him but Georgi's illness, it took a moment to remember that Cassie had been a pretender to his hand. "Oh!" He frowned, noted his guest's twinkling eyes, and relaxed. "You jest, of course, although how you can, I don't know."

"I'll admit I'm getting a little of my own back. Thanks to Georgi's accident, I am trapped with my daughter-in-law and her tirades against a scheming wench who persists in doing all she can to put herself forward, even to pretending illness . . ." He broke off, his brow rising. "I think you see the picture? You wish to marry Georgi, do you not? *Not* poor little Cassie who is so despondent she barely hears one speak to her, suffering from a broken heart, according to her mother, because you have ceased your attentions to her. I think," went on his lordship, thoughtfully, "I must soon allow her to visit Georgi. Even if she can't see her cousin, she'll very likely come in contact with Sedgewycke who," he added in irritation, "I'm led to understand, does everything but stand on his head to avoid anyone seeing him. Perhaps he will put a little heart into the nitwit."

"You approved his suit?"

"Yes. My son is in consultation with the lawyers. Settlements, you know. The two of them are that sure of little Cassie. I've had a letter from him which I'll hand to his wife at the appropriate moment. Assuming Cassie doesn't surprise us all and refuse him."

"And the other romance? Does it progress?"

"You know of Elliot's pursuit of the widow?" Tivington chuckled. "I have come to like our little widow. She has a sense of humor and can even laugh at her own oddities which include her excessive preoccupation with her fortune. Laughing at them doesn't mean she'll give them up, one must understand. Merely, it means she is not a bore about them. She has saved me more than once from strangling my daughter-in-law and already has Elliot under the cat's paw to a degree, not that Melicent gives credit where it is due. She insists it is because of her maternal influence he no longer sneaks off to the village and has begun drinking less than was his wont. The match will prosper, even if Elliot never realizes he has come to love the widow almost as much as he loves her gold!"

"You think he does?"

"I think that for the first time in Elliot's misspent life, he is thinking of another before himself. It will be the making of him."

"His temper . . ."

"She has the happy talent of defusing his temper before it builds too far. She makes him laugh."

"Once he discovers she will hold the reins, will he still laugh?"

"She understands that buying her way back into the *ton* is a costly process," responded Tivington dryly. "She will not stint when agreeing to his allowance although she suggests that he have it monthly instead of quarterly in the hopes he'll do a bit better budgeting it!"

Lord Tivington managed to keep a sober mien while repeating his latest discussion with the widow, but he had the misfortune of looking sideways at Lord Everhart as he finished. Everhart was looking at him in the same manner. The two fell into guffaws, which had Anne rushing out into the corridor.

"Quiet!" she hissed. "We have managed to get Georgi to fall into a proper sleep, and you will rouse her with your idiotic and thoughtless riot and rumpus."

"She is better?" asked Everhart, sobering instantly. A brilliant smile lit Anne's tired face and Everhart saw her as she had been in her youth. He wondered, idly, why, when she must have been a beauty, she'd been left on the shelf.

"My niece is on the mend. The fever broke an hour ago and she sleeps but—" She returned to her frowning self. "—she is weak and in a condition where she might catch her death of something else if not carefully guarded, which she will be. But for the moment go away, the both of you. Georgi will not thank you for waking her and neither will the rest of us," she finished with a yawn. Anne returned to the bedroom, closing the door with a snap.

"I guess that's telling us," said Everhart quietly, a smile he couldn't repress making the words a joke.

"My Georgina Anne has always a sharp tongue to her. But she means well." Lord Tivington compressed his lips and shook his head, a sad little movement hinting at much. "Yes, she does. Even when she cut off her own nose to spite her face, she meant well."

Lord Everhart stared at the door for a long moment, wondering again about Anne Beverly but believed,

rightly, that Lord Tivington's words were all he'd ever
learn in answer to his curiosity concerning Miss Anne
Beverly's past. At that moment his stomach rumbled
and he looked down his length in bewilderment. "I feel
as if I haven't eaten for a week."

Hamish, hearing his cue, left off his eavesdropping
and entered the hall. "Not a week. A mere three days.
Now come along with you, do! Alphonse will fix you a
nice little omelet as only he knows how to do and slice
ham from the one he brought down from London. You'll
eat breakfast today, unlike what you've been doing,
which is to drink your meal." He scolded in similar
fashion all the way down the stairs.

Lord Tivington's brow snapped up as he watched
them go, wondering that Lord Everhart did not reprimand his servant. He followed the two men. Everhart
grinned ruefully when he turned to ask if Lord Tivington would join him in the breakfast room. "It is one of
the few rooms in this house which I like. There are
many windows and a light-colored wallpaper which
does not offend. The furniture is unbelievably beautiful
Queen Anne. I am told it was part of Sir Minnow's
wife's dowry and the one thing he insisted be cared for
while the rest of the house went to rack and ruin."

Tivington allowed himself to be talked into joining
his lordship in a bite to eat and a good pint of home
brew for, if truth be told, he, too, had been picking at his
food the last few days.

"You've a strange man for servant," he said, when
they'd been served and Hamish left the room.

Everhart took a moment to understand what Lord
Tivington could mean. "Oh. You mean his scolding. We
have become very close, my lord, which is not common
between man and servant. Hamish and I traveled far to
strange places and have been in tight squeezes where

we've had to rely entirely on each other. One forms a bond . . ."

"One does indeed. I had a groom who played much the same role in my life although he kept his place when others were around!"

"Hamish is not himself. He has worried about me as I've worried about Georgi."

When he didn't go on Lord Tivington nodded and, politely, changed the subject.

Late that night Georgi grew restless. Her eyes fluttered, opened, stared up at the blood red tester in which the fire light caught threads of gold. She turned her head. To the side a large chair was set close to the bed. Someone sat there. Muzzily, Georgi tried to determine who it might be. Someone large and comforting, that she knew. Someone she'd dreamed about during the days of her illness . . .

Illness. She'd been ill. Yes. Now she remembered. Aunt Anne had explained she'd been brought to Lord Everhart's house, where she still lay. "Thirsty," she muttered.

The figure in the chair turned its head to look toward the fire where a lounge chair had been set. The sleeping person there snored lightly, so the man leaned forward and stood. "I'll get your barley water, Georgi," he said softly. "One moment, my dear."

Everhart? He was sitting by her bed in the middle of the night? Oh dear. Georgi fiddled her hands out from under the covers, and raised them to her hair. She brushed it back, discovered her hands were incredibly weak, and decided it didn't matter. But it *did*. "I must look a mess," she said, when he returned and carefully lifted her so she could drink.

"To me you look more beautiful than all the flowers

in May. You are *alive*. You can't know, my Georgi, how I feared we'd lose you."

"I'm very difficult to be rid of, my lord," she said when she'd drunk and he'd laid her back onto newly fluffed pillows. She regretted his arm was no longer around her, that his dear face was where she could barely see him in the shadows. "Ask Grandfather. He has had more chances than he likes to know that."

"If you mean you have been ill too often, I know." He glanced toward the sleeping figure which, at his hard tone, turned, resettled itself, and slept on. When he leaned forward to speak again his voice was lower but still intense. "Georgi, I've discovered I love you very much. I'd decided not to speak of it to you now because you must have a Season, must not be charmed or pressured as I and your grandfather could easily do, into giving your dear hand to me before you see something of the world. I'm not asking that, even now, but I cannot be silent. I must tell you how I feel and that I hope, someday, to make you my wife. It will be the hardest thing I've ever done, watching you have your Season, watching you meet interesting men who will adore you, watching you learn your power and see you develop the charm and poise you'll achieve as you lose the lovely innocence of a green girl. I'll hate that loss, but I'll admire the woman I know you'll become and, where the green girl would eventually pall, the woman will only grow in grace and interest." The gentle clasp he'd taken of her thin hand tightened. He leaned still farther forward until his head rested against their entwined hands.

"You've spoken to Grandfather?" she asked, her heart pounding. He was the Prince's man and Grandfather the King's. To whom must she be loyal?

"Yes. He's been generous in his approval of me."

Georgi's eyes widened, and a sigh of relief drifted from her barely opened lips.

"But that approval," he added, "may be because I suggested we wait . . . Georgi, Georgi, my love, can I bear it?"

"I don't see why you must," she breathed, her eyes glowing, her gaze resting on his tousled hair. Tentatively she raised her other hand. Softly she touched it, moved a strand into place, then, daringly, ran her fingers into it, letting her palm follow the shape of his skull. He raised his head, letting her fingers trail to where his neck and shoulder met. Their gaze fused, his asking, hers innocently revealing the feeling which had been building and building within her.

Very slowly he lowered his head until their lips met. Very carefully he retained control of his passions so as not to frighten her. *Besides,* he reminded himself, as he backed away, *she has been ill. She is not yet out of the woods.* Retaining her hand, he sat back into his chair and the "sleeping" figure closed the eye which had been monitoring the pair. Nanny settled herself. She'd heard Everhart was an honorable man. Now she actually believed it. The low murmur of voices was a lullaby which soon put her back to sleep. She only woke again when Everhart rose to his feet:

"I must leave you, Georgi. You must sleep and get well."

"I think our conversation will do more to make me well than all the sleep in the world. I love you."

"And I you. I will talk with your grandfather tomorrow."

Georgi chuckled softly. "I thought you had."

"Oh yes. That I might properly court you. Well, I guess, despite my excellent intentions, the courting is done. Now I must ask permission to send in the notice of our engagement and discuss with him how soon we may plan a wedding." Everhart chuckled. "I had an odd letter from Prince George last week. I couldn't make heads or tails of it then, but now I do. You must have impressed him a great deal, my love, and matchmaker that he is, he'll insist he planned our union. In his letter he said he'll enjoy attending my wedding. Now I'll have to write and tell him when and where."

Nanny's eyes blinked open. Prince George? Wedding! Just what had happened while she slept! She roused herself and forced her limbs to move. "My lord? Why are you here?"

"I'm going," he said, raising Georgi's hand in both of his to place a kiss in its palm. He closed her fingers around it, lay her hand down, and backed away. "I'm going, Nanny. Don't look around for a willow switch. I'll be good."

"Good and sassy, you mean," grumbled Nanny, drawing on her old robe. She walked stiffly to the bedside spot he'd vacated. Georgi, she noted, followed his progress from the room, just the corners of her lips tipping and her eyes lightening. Then the girl smiled. It was one of Georgi's more glorious smiles, which was saying a great deal when even her ordinary ones glowed with life and happiness. "You may wish me happy, Nanny. We are engaged."

"He had the infernal gall to ask you to marry him while you lay on your sickbed?"

"Oh no. He only declared his feelings for me, telling me he could not bear that I not know, that while I was so ill he'd feared he'd never have the chance to tell me and that he'd promised himself he would at first opportunity."

"So he snuck into a lady's bedchamber when she was

defenseless and wormed his way into her confidence, did he?"

"No," said Georgi with another of those smiles, although this one had much of the old mischief in it. "I had to offer for him."

"You proposed to Lord Everhart?"

"I had to. It became clear the idiotic man was going to insist on remaining honorably aloof while I looked over all the eligibles the Season had to offer. He claims there is a marquess who is better-looking and younger and who would indulge me to the top of my bent. In fact, he'd join in all my escapades and very likely lead me to my death and at that point my lord scowled, bit his lip, and turned away from me." Georgi chuckled. "It took some coaxing to convince him I had no ambitions toward becoming a marchioness. He seemed to think I'd like this marquess excessively, you see."

"And would you not?"

"Very likely. But I won't love him," said Georgi serenely. "I couldn't. Not when I love Everhart with everything within me."

"I don't suppose I should have allowed such goings-on. Lady Anne will have kitty fits," mumbled Nanny, studying her charge. She went on to tuck Georgi's arms back under the covers and to smooth her pillows. "Well, there, child. All this excitement when you should be sleeping. I'll go make you a nice soothing draught and you rest while I do it, do you hear me?"

"Nanny, truly it is not necessary. I am already feeling sleepy. Let me sleep naturally, Nanny. I do not like that laudanum. It does nasty things to my head."

Nanny nodded. "I don't like it either but as a composer there is nothing which will match it. Your aunt insisted and I agreed sleep was necessary so we used it, but now . . ." She studied Georgi through narrowed eyes.

"Very well. Try and sleep. If you can, then I'll not give it you."

Georgi closed her eyes, her mind drifting back to that very gentle kiss. Suddenly her eyes popped open. *Allowed such goings on!* What had Nanny meant by that? *Allowed?* Had the old dear seen that kiss? Yes, very likely she had. Georgi forced her limbs to relax. Whatever Nanny had seen, she would say nothing, so all was well. Again Georgi allowed her senses to remember Lord Everhart's stolen kiss. It was, she thought, all a first kiss should be, holding gentle but sure promise of so much more. Smiling, Georgi drifted back to sleep.

Everhart would never forget the kiss by the river, but Georgi, already succumbing to her illness at the time, never did remember it—much to her disgust.

Several days later everyone returned to the Place. Georgi had not fully regained her old strength, but it was returning rapidly as it always did. Her aunts were glad to be home in their own rooms and Aunt Marie went to hers, not to appear again for nearly thirty-six hours. Much of that time she slept, telling everyone who would listen she never slept well except in her own bed. Anne was no sooner out of the coach than she was off to check the succession houses and then what the gardeners had been up to in the flower beds while she was gone. She muttered about the taking up of the bulbs and corms as she went. . . .

Grandfather took charge of Georgi, leading her into the study, where he had had a chaise longue placed for her convenience. "You will not like to go to your bed after just escaping one, but you are not yet strong enough you may do just as you please. Here I may monitor your visitors and see you are not overtaxed. And here is the first of them. Mrs. Compton, you are looking well."

"And a miracle it is that I am. You can't know how pleased I am you have all come home again. And I *should* say how happy I am you are looking so well, Miss Georgi. But I'm on my head or my heels with keeping that Elliot of yours in line, Lord Tivington. It will have to be soon now . . ." She tossed a speculative look toward Georgi.

"You've a plan?" she asked.

"Yes. If I can work it properly. It required your grandfather, you see, and with him at the Manor so much, I've had to play poor Elty like a fish. *He* don't know where he is either!"

Georgi chuckled. "Grandfather tells me poor Elliot is in love."

"I think he is, poor boy. Not that he knows it. And you aren't to tell him, either. He'll never guess it, thinking such things twaddle, you know. But he'll be much easier for me to manage so long as I can keep him in a dither. Do you think this evening too soon, my lord?"

Lord Tivington pulled his watch from his fob. He tipped his head and the eyebrow arched as he looked at Georgi. "Mrs. Compton, I believe it just the thing to perk up our invalid. We have several hours before dinner which Georgi will have in her bed so she may go to sleep early. If you were to run your rig *now,* she could be entertained by it, think you so?"

Mrs. Compton pursed her lips. "He's easier to trick when he's had a glass or two with dinner, but perhaps I can manage it. I'll take him for a walk in the garden and we'll see what I can do. 'Bye now."

Alicia ran Elliot to earth in the billiard room. He suggested a game and she suggested a walk. She gave him a sidelong look which immediately had him thinking thoughts of unbridled passion amongst the rhododendron bushes and he allowed her to lead him away. The useful bower was empty, something Alicia had not been able to count on since it was a favorite spot for Cassie's mooning. "Here we are," she said, seating herself.

"Yes," he muttered, carefully glancing around to see that they were alone before ducking under the low, vine-covered, entrance. He saw Alicia had chosen a chair instead of the cushioned bench and frowned. "Yes," he said, "here we are. Only you are over there and I'm over here and that's not at all the way I like it, you know."

"Bad boy!" She batted her slightly darkened lashes at him and thought, with affectionate humor, that if he were a dog his tongue would be hanging out. " 'Tis the middle of the day and you'd look a fine fool if we were caught misbehaving, now wouldn't you?"

Elliot, thinking of all the ways he'd like to misbehave with the illusive widow, abandoned the bench for his knees at her side. He clutched her hands between his damp palms. "Mrs. Compton . . . Alicia . . . you know how much I wish to please you . . ."

"Thought myself, it was me pleasing you you had in mind," she said, but with enough coyness she didn't give offense.

He nodded several times. "That too. We could, you know. Please each other. If you would . . ." He gulped, readying himself to make his offer of a nice little house in Chelsea—but never got the chance.

"Would?" Alicia jumped to her feet, drawing him up with her. "Would? But, Elty, I thought you'd never ask. Oh, we must hurry. At once, Elty." She tugged the bewildered young man out of the bower and, talking all the way, led them to the French doors to the library.

Lord Tivington, on the watch, saw them coming and had them open before the pair reached them. "Why, how bright and happy you look, Mrs. Compton. Have you good news for us?"

"I hope you'll not object, my lord, but Elty here, just proposed and I've accepted and we wanted you to be the first to know."

Elliot's mouth dropped open. He shook his head, tried to back away, but was held in a viselike grip by his fianceé.

"Congratulations, grandson! I never thought you'd have such good sense!"

Elliot blinked. Good sense? He stopped trying to escape, curious. Alicia, at a look from Lord Tivington and the jerk of the old man's head, released her grip a trifle reluctantly. She moved to where Georgi lay trying to contain giggles at the expression on her cousin's face.

"After losing all that money," said Grandfather softly, "I thought you'd merely pout and expect someone else to take care of it for you, but here you've gone and won yourself a very rich lady who will, I'm certain, settle with your father like a gentleman. You *gay dog* you!"

Gay dog, was he? Settle, would she? Ah yes, the Golden Widow . . . Somehow, somewhere along the line, Elliot had lost track of that exceedingly pertinent detail. She was rich. And she wanted to marry him. So she must be head over heels in love with him, which meant he should have no trouble wringing a great deal of money from her clutches. It also occurred to him, that as her husband, he should have control of her fortune. Which meant . . . Visions crowded Elliot's head of nights of debauchery and gaming and races and all the things he'd longed to join in on but had been unable to do because the dibs were never in tune—even though he'd run up debts trying.

"M'father'll be pleased," he said tentatively. Lord Tivington nodded agreement.

Then Elliot thought of his mother. His mother did not like the widow. She had, in fact, on more than one occasion, had words with Grandfather concerning the continued presence of the woman under the old man's roof. Vulgar was about the nicest of the terms Lady Melicent had used to describe her.

"M'mother won't like it at all," he said. "Might as well forget the whole thing."

"You leave your mother to me, Elliot. I'll make it right and tight with her!" *And enjoy doing it,* thought Lord Tivington, who had never liked his daughter-in-law as one should. *In fact,* he thought, *very likely I'll like Mrs. Compton—despite her undoubted vulgarity—far better than I've ever liked Melicent.* "I'll deal with your mother."

"With m'mother?" Elliot looked at his grandfather, his face a picture of surprise. "No one deals with m'mother!"

"I can. Come along now." He took his grandson by the elbow and led him to where Alicia and Georgi spoke quietly. "We'll have to have a celebration to announce your engagement. How soon do you think you could handle a small party, Georgi?"

"You mean when will I feel like it? You know how rapidly I return to my normal good health. Tomorrow night would be fine if it can be arranged so quickly. Or how about an alfresco party the following afternoon? The nights become chill but the days are still lovely. We can set trestles on the terrace where Aunt Anne's dahlias are at the height of their glory. The announcement can be made in front of them. If you wear your pale green gown, Alicia, and Elliot that matching green vest . . ." She raised her eyes to meet Alicia's and they smiled.

"That would be very nice, I think. And you will not be tired as you might if we were to plan an evening party."

A knock turned all heads toward the French doors,

where Everhart stood, looking around as if he feared he might be seen. He slipped inside as soon as the door was opened. "I just missed running into Miss Beverly."

"Your quick reflexes saved you, however," soothed Lord Tivington. "Everhart, you must be the first beyond ourselves to learn of the engagement between Mrs. Compton and my grandson."

"I wish you very happy, Mrs. Compton, and congratulate you, you lucky man, on choosing a lovely bride."

"She is rather lovely, ain't she," said Elliot, a trifle surprised. He couldn't seem to keep more than one thing in his head at a time. At the moment Everhart spoke, he'd been thinking of Alicia's fortune and wondering how soon he could make a touch at it. He'd forgotten his equally strong desire to have a touch at the widow herself, but now couldn't keep his eyes decently off her figure!

"You lovebirds will have all sorts of things to say to each other, I'm sure," said Lord Tivington. "You run along. I'll tell Marie she is to arrange the party immediately. You are free, are you not, my lord, in the afternoon, the day after tomorrow?"

"Of course." As the newly engaged couple left the room he asked, "Now how did you manage *that?*"

"Alicia did it," said Georgi. "How I wish I might have been there. She tells me Elliot was on his knees, having built up his courage to make his nasty offer of a little house in Chelsea when she caught him up and made *him* believe *she* believed he'd made a proposal of quite a different nature. She dragged him in here to announce it before he could get a word in to deny it. Grandfather then took him in hand and reminded Elliot the widow is rich. He immediately accepted his fate."

"Poor lad." Grandfather shook his head in mock sadness. "He'll never know how he was manipulated, or how long, thanks to Georgi's accident, he was held on a tight rein and not allowed to give her the slip on the shoulder he'd intended." His lordship shook his head.

Everhart looked quickly to his love but she was equally amused and not the least upset by a subject he felt she should know nothing about or if she *did,* should find disgusting or embarrassing or both. The door opened and Vincent stepped into the room. Everhart remembered who had been responsible for Georgi's unconventional education about things she should not know and glowered.

"What have I done now?" asked Vincent, coming closer.

"I'll explain it to you later," growled Everhart, sidling closer to Georgi, who put up her hand. He grasped it firmly, possessively, and watched her cousin's brows rise in sharp arcs. "Georgi has done me the honor of accepting my proposal."

"What happened to all that high-minded nonsense of allowing her her Season before you stepped in to claim her?" asked Vincent with a certain irritating insouciance.

Georgi frowned. "I can't think where he got such a foolish notion." She shook her head, her lips compressed. "Foolish beyond permission as anyone with any sense would agree. Why should we waste so much time? Oh, were you unaware, Grandfather, that we had finally managed to communicate our feelings to each other?"

"When?" he asked, his bluntness having an edge of danger to it. Georgi and Everhart looked at each other. Georgi bit her lip, trying to repress giggles. Everhart flushed more deeply. "I see," said Tivington dryly. *"More* irregular behavior. I suppose we cannot call you out since the *result* is honorable . . ."

"But it isn't. I mean, I should not have offered for her until she has seen more of the world. She may think that foolish, but how can she be sure of her feelings until . . . It is just that . . ."

"That you nearly lost her altogether and the thought was unbearable. I'll have to have a word with Nanny. The woman is obviously becoming too old for the duties entrusted to her."

Georgi blushed this time. "She has not. She merely played the role of any good chaperone and made sure that nothing of an . . . an immoral nature took place."

"Not so much as a kiss?" asked Vincent. "Slowtop," he added, sotto voce.

"You and I," said Everhart equally softly, "will have to come to some agreement. You'll be seeing more of Georgi in future and I'll not have you leading her down any of the many garden paths which litter a green girl's path in London."

"Me lead *her?"* said Vincent, offended. "It's far more likely she'll be leading me. She always has in the past, anyway."

Thoughtfully, Everhart looked at his bride-to-be. "In future she leads me or no one, understand?"

Vincent chuckled. "Brat, are you listening? I warn you, Everhart, she is already plotting ways of dispensing with society's rigid rules."

"Don't encourage her," said Lord Tivington. "She may have come up with the notions for the escapades you two fell into whenever you stayed here, but I've always believed it was you, George Vincent, who made the plans work. Georgi, you will have to become respectable and that is all there is to it."

He saw her glance toward her desk, a frown on her brow.

"And that is another thing! Lord Everhart, I wish a

long talk with you before I agree you may have my granddaughter's hand! There are things you must know and, equally, attitudes on your part which *she* must know. You are not to discuss your agreement with anyone until I am assured it will come to pass. George Vincent, do you hear me?"

"I never tell tales. You are thinking of Elliot."

"I will talk with Lord Everhart now. Vincent, you take Georgi up to her room. She needs rest. Georgi, do not frown so. I feel sure you need not concern yourself, but you know full well where problems may lie."

"Grandfather," said Vincent softly, "have you ever attended one of the dowager Lady Everhart's literary evenings? If not I suggest you begin by asking Lord Everhart about them. Georgi will enjoy them very much." He held out his hand to help her rise. "Come along, brat. I'll give you a game of piquet so you need not worry about what is going on here. We'll be in the old sewing room, Grandfather, if you want us."

"Grandfather," said Georgi as she was pulled from the room, "you have not forgotten a party must be arranged?"

"I'll have a message sent to your aunt that she's to begin and that I'll explain later. Run along child. I've your best interests at heart even if you think not at this moment." Georgi threw one slightly anguished look toward the desk, another toward Everhart, and stared at her cousin. Vincent nodded encouragingly, and with one deep sigh, she closed the door behind them.

"Now," said Lord Tivington, going to a bookcase where a shelf was devoted to novels of the more lurid sort of Gothic, "are you familiar with this type of reading which seems to have swept the *ton* these last few years?"

"I have read a few of them myself," admitted Everhart, his eyes narrowing. "My mother has met most of the authors and encouraged those she believes merit it."

Tivington straightened, two sets of volumes in his hands. "Vincent mentioned your mother's salon. She is an authoress herself?"

"She has published a volume of her poetry. It has received some thoughtful reviews."

It was Tivington's turn for narrowed eyes. "She'd be tolerant of a writer's foibles then. Are *you,* my lord?" He hefted the volumes and held them out.

Everhart took them and looked at the titles. "I have read this one. It was well designed, I thought, and better written than many. I have not seen the other. Is it new?"

"It has been out for only a month. The volumes were sent to me by messenger as soon as they left the bindery."

"Why?"

"Have you not guessed?"

"They are Georgi's."

"She has another very nearly finished. It is not a hobby with her. She writes because she must."

"You are saying that as my wife she will not stop her scribbling. I will be proud to support her efforts." He grinned. "So will my mother."

Tivington turned to a chair and seated himself heavily. "You said this was better written than many. I believe it is because she is far better educated than most women, a bluestocking if you will." Again there was challenge in the tone.

"I had guessed she had tendencies in that direction, my lord," said Everhart gently. "You see, one of the things that drew me to her was that she did not bore me with talk of fashion or the latest *on dit.* She knew the references a man lets fall into his conversation and, once or twice, she topped them. It is well. *She* will not wish to prattle nonsense when I've settled before the fire with a dollop of brandy and a new book, hoping for a quiet sensible evening."

"She is far more likely to ask for her own glass and become engrossed in her own reading. She will, I warn, become irritated if you are a restless sort of reader, always moving around in your chair or poking at the fire . . ."

". . . or getting up to freshen my glass or to look up another reference." Everhart tipped his head. "I do that last, you know. Hunt for passages in other books which are referred to in my current reading."

"Georgi has an incredible memory. She will help you track them down. Now that we have settled that so agreeably, you'd best tell Georgi she may stop worrying and concentrate on her cards so that Vincent will not end by strangling her." Everhart was told the way to the sewing room and started out, only to be caught by Lady Melicent. He was only able to get away by telling Cassie's mother he'd dropped by to ask after Georgi's health. "She is better?" he asked.

"Oh yes. But you will not leave before you've said hello to my Cassandra, surely."

"I fear I must. I've very little time before meeting a man about . . . about repairing the bridge that caused the problem. Lord Tivington and I were to consult on it, you see, and we have, but it took too long and now I must run . . ." As he spoke, he backed away from her down the hall, slipped back into the library where he mopped his brow, and glowered at Lord Tivington, who had overheard much of the discussion and was laughing. Everhart exited via the French doors to the garden just as Lady Melicent followed him into the library.

"I don't understand that man," said Lady Melicent, frowning lightly.

"What's to understand? He wants to avoid you and your daughter and does the best he can to be polite about it. You make it damned difficult for him to do so, do you not?"

"You don't know what you are saying."

"Don't I just! Melicent, you are due a fall. I will enjoy helping you to it." He frowned crossly and told her to go away and leave him in peace—"And, since you're going anyway, you might as well make yourself useful and send Georgia Marie in to me. Instantly."

Twelve

It was a glorious early autumn afternoon. The beeches had only begun to turn, the sun was high in a blue sky, and on the sheltered terrace stylishly dressed women didn't worry about catching a chill. A chaise longue had been placed strategically for Georgi, but she had to be reminded by all and sundry to return to it. Everhart's Alphonse had contributed to the buffet meal, which was lavish and well wetted by wines and ale and lemonade. Grandfather had decided to produce some of his treasured and irreplaceable champagne for the toast to the announcements, not that Melicent knew this was more than a party to celebrate Georgi's recovery. She was loud in her complaints it was merely spoiling the girl to do such a silly thing.

Everyone was mellow and happy when Grandfather took his place and called his grandchildren close. Lord Everhart was among those who drew near. Having escorted Georgi on a gentle walk, he brought her to Lord Tivington's side . . . and stayed there.

"I have announcements to make. Several happy announcements," said Lord Tivington. "My son has written me concerning his children, both Georgette Cassandra and my grandson, George Elliot. My son is at this moment discussing settlements with various lawyers."

Melicent blinked. *Both* her children? But why was

Everhart still standing close to Georgi and wasn't that the despised brother of the much despised widow whispering to Cassie and making her blush. Melicent bit her lip. Something was happening which she didn't understand and instinctively knew she wouldn't like. She glanced around, wondering what she could do to stop whatever mischief her father-in-law was promulgating. He was looking at her and had that gleam in his eyes she distrusted! She must *do* something!

"First," said Lord Tivington, "my granddaughter Georgette Cassandra and Aaron Sedgewycke will be married in three weeks time at the local church. You are all, of course, invited." His eyes narrowed and he held his daughter-in-law's look, daring her to say a word. She gasped, her hand going to her heaving bosom. "Second, George Elliot Beverly has been a very lucky man indeed to gain the hand of Mrs. Alicia Compton. Their vows will be taken during the Little Season in London at St. George's in Hanover Square. Again, you are all welcome."

Murmurs were running through the crowd by this time and Melicent was almost steaming with anger and resentment. How dare her father-in-law manage her family in this high-handed fashion! *What of Everhart?* He was Cassie's chosen husband, and surely no one with any sense would actually welcome that encroaching and vulgar widow into their family! What could she *do?*

"I said I had several announcements. The third is the engagement of Lord Everhart and my beloved Georgi. They met this summer and have, without anyone knowing, fallen deeply and completely in love. I am very pleased to announce they too will be married this fall during the Little Season. Their wish that they be married here had to be set aside due to the wishes of our Prince. Our Prince met my Georgi this summer in Brighton. He sent his friend Everhart a matchmaking message. Prince George couldn't know he was already behind the times when he suggested his old friend, Everhart, should make the acquaintance of his new friend, Miss Beverly—he ends his missive by hinting that it will please him to attend the ceremony in Hanover Square, which he knows will result from their meeting. We have no choice in the matter. I'm sorry, Georgi, that your wedding must be postponed." He looked around, noted Melicent had passed out on Georgi's chaise, decided she looked comfortable enough, and smiled gently at his guests. "Champagne is being served. Will you join us in toasts to our three couples? George Vincent? Will you do the honors."

Lord Tivington took a moment to tuck her husband's letter into Melicent's décolletage. She opened one eye and glared at him; he smiled wolfishly, silently telling her the day toward which he'd looked had arrived. When she flushed an ugly puce, he turned away to attend Vincent.

Vincent stepped forward. He raised his glass and silence fell. "May my cousin Cassie live long and well and may my friend Aaron never regret his choice!" Vincent's insouciance took the sting from his words. Even Cassie chuckled.

Vincent grinned at Elliot, whose expression immediately took on a wary look. "May my cousin Elliot live long and well and may Mrs. Compton not regret *her* choice!" Elliot gritted his teeth but managed a smile even though the laughter took on a different note.

There was one more toast. "I need not wish either of this pair happiness for I know they'll have it in abundance. I'll wish them a long and loving life, however, since I'm also certain neither will regret the choice they've made." Vincent smiled. "All the very best, brat," he added softly.

"Amen," breathed Lord Tivington just as softly.

"Amen, amen," whispered Georgi and Everhart together, their gaze full on each other's faces. Everhart's gaze dropped to Georgi's lips. She blushed.

No one quite knew why, but there was much happy laughter and the exciting day ran on. What's more, it didn't tire Georgi one bit—although Melicent soon found it necessary to retire to her room.

A CONFOUNDING FEMALE

Miss Georgianna Beverly is quite content with her life just as it is. Happily unshackled, she is free to pursue her secret talent as an author of popular poetry. Certainly she is not *opposed* to love, in fact, she is quite skilled in the art of matchmaking for her sisters and cousins. But what man would ever want to wed such a contrary miss as herself —a dedicated bluestocking who would rather debate politics than dance; who prefers the company of books over simpering husband-hungry females?

A CONFIRMED BACHELOR

Lord Everhart had nothing in mind but a scheme of mutual convenience when he first set eyes on the sprite of a girl whose quick intelligence belied her youthful appearance. Though Georgi is not concerned with the ways of the *ton*, she happily agrees to help him foil the scheming ape leaders determined to see him wed. While their sham courtship raises eyebrows, no one is more stunned than his lordship when he realizes that somewhere in this charade, he has completely lost his heart. Now, he must persuade Georgi to do the same...

Visit us at www.kensingtonbooks.com

07566>

0 71268 00499 4

ISBN 0-8217-7566-9

ZEBRA
U.S.$4.99
CAN $6.99